Frank Viva

SEA
CHANGE

FOR BARBARA ANN VIVA

{ Editorial Director: Françoise Mouly
Editor: Nadja Spiegelman
Design: Frank Viva
Frank Viva's artwork was drawn in pencil
and india ink and colored digitally. }

FOR VISUAL READERS
TOON
GRAPHICS

A JUNIOR LIBRARY GUILD SELECTION

©2016 Frank Viva & TOON Books, an imprint of RAW Junior, LLC,
27 Greene Street, New York, NY 10013.
No part of this book may be used or reproduced in any manner whatsoever without written permission except in the case of brief
quotations embodied in critical articles and reviews. TOON Graphics™, TOON Books®, LITTLE LIT® and TOON Into Reading!™
are trademarks of RAW Junior, LLC. All rights reserved. The text was set in FF Scala, an old style, humanist, serif typeface
designed in 1990 by Martin Majoor. The display lettering was hand-drawn by Frank Viva. Cover by Frank Viva.
All of our books are Smyth Sewn (the highest library-quality binding available) and printed with soy-based inks on acid-free, wood-
free paper harvested from responsible sources. Printed in China by C&C Offset Printing Co., Ltd.
Distributed to the trade by Consortium Book Sales and Distribution, Inc.; orders (800) 283-3572 34;
orderentry@perseusbooks.com; www.cbsd.com.
Library of Congress Cataloging-in-Publication Data:
Viva, Frank, author, illustrator. Sea change: a Toon graphic / Frank Viva. pages cm
Summary : "Follows a young boy who is sent to spend the summer in a remote part of Nova Scotia against his will.
As the summer wears on, the hero forges solid friendships with other kids in the small fishing community
and is changed forever by the experience"– Provided by publisher.
ISBN 978-1-935179-92-4 (hardcover : alk. paper)
[1. Friendship--Fiction. 2. Coming of age--Fiction. 3. Summer--Fiction. 4. Nova Scotia--Fiction. 5. Canada--Fiction.] I. Title.
PZ7.7.V59Se 2016   741.5'973--dc23   2015029061
16 17 18 19 20 21 C&C 10 9 8 7 6 5 4 3 2 1
TOON-BOOKS.com

1

It was the last day of school, the best day of school. I was walking home between my two best friends, Mike and Teddy. They laughed and cracked jokes, but I was quiet. For Mike and Teddy, the whole everlasting summer stretched ahead of them, filled with promise. For me, it hung in the sky like a big question mark. Mike and Teddy had normal parents who didn't try to mess up their lives, but my parents were different. My parents were dumping me with relatives in Nova Scotia for the summer.

Here is pretty much everything I knew about Nova Scotia:

• It was about a million miles away from Lakefield.

• The entire province was filled with wrinkly old relatives who smelled like fish.

"You'll probably get eaten by a yeti," said Mike.

"Or a great white shark," said Teddy. He grabbed my arm and pretended to bite it.

I had worked twelve long years to get to this summer, and my parents were throwing it away like chopped liver. Even worse, I had to listen in silence as Mike and Teddy described the hundred

and one fun things they would be doing while I was getting torn to pieces at the far end of Canada. I wouldn't be there for the backyard sleepover. I wouldn't hear the ghost stories told by flashlight in our canvas pup tents. I wouldn't be invited by Teddy's mom to come with them in the big station wagon to the drive-in movies. I wouldn't help make the merry-go-round at the drive-in playground go so fast that you couldn't hold on. There would be no intermission with hot dogs and french fries for me. Mike and Teddy would walk up to Lucky's Variety to buy monster cards and the latest issue of Spiderman. Without me. They would go down to Black Creek and cross over the muddy river on our rope swing to spy on the rich kids at the old Simpson house. Without me. They would add a lookout to our tree house, hauling the scraps of wood up with our rope and pulley. Without me. They would go on all the rides at the shopping mall carnival, buy Cherry Bombs and Jimmie Cones from the ice cream man, catch pollywogs in jam jars...all without me.

Both my parents were to blame for this tragedy, but my insane mother was the true mastermind behind it all.

"You'll love it," she kept saying. "When I was your age I spent an entire summer in Point Aconi, and it was the best summer of my life." Point Aconi? That didn't even sound like the name of a real place.

"Sounds like the name of a sharp object to me," I said. "Sounds dangerous."

My mother just laughed at me. The crazy woman actually thought she was doing me a favor. She even showed me an old black-and-white photograph of herself in a swimsuit, smiling next to some boys. "See?" she said.

"See what?"

"See what a great time I had?"

What did I care if some stupid girl I'd never met had a great time at some stupid place over a hundred years ago? But I didn't say that out loud. I just went up to my room and shut the door. I stayed there for the next two days, refusing to talk to anybody. When my mother knocked on the door and said that Mike and Teddy wanted me to come out and play, I told her to tell them I was dead. I would have preferred to be dead rather than be reminded of all the things I was going to miss. I pulled the covers over my head and turned up the volume on my radio.

Soon, I would be flying in an airplane, to a place I didn't know, to work for a crabby old man I didn't know. He was my grandmother's brother, so he must be crabby. Wouldn't my parents be sorry if the plane crashed? "Why, why, why did we send him?" my mother would cry.

"Because you're the meanest mother in the world," my ghost would answer spookily.

I couldn't imagine things getting any worse. Then I saw the beach towel with the girly pink mermaid on it. "What's that?" I asked.

"It's your new beach towel, honey," said my mom.

The idea of dying on the plane no longer interested me, because it wasn't soon enough. I wanted to die right then and there. The large green suitcase from the basement was sitting open on my bed like a giant mouth about to swallow me. It was almost time to go.

"Sweetie," she said, "you're going to have the time of your life. Trust me." Trust her? I was supposed to trust the mother who bought me a beach towel with a pink mermaid on it?

"Time to go," said my sister, Joan. "Don't worry, little brother, I'll take good care of your bedroom while you're gone."

"You'd better not go into my room or you're dead," I said. "If I see one thing out of place you're in big trouble. I'll tell your boyfriend that you smell bad and have armpit hair!"

"Harold and I broke up yesterday, little brother, so you can tell him whatever you want."

"Kids, it's time to go!" my father yelled from the front door.

As the car pulled out of the driveway, I saw Mike and Teddy waving from Teddy's front lawn. I slid down in my seat and pretended not to see them. After we turned the corner at the top of our street, I felt terrible. I folded my arms and refused to talk to anybody. When we got to the highway I had a sick feeling in the pit of my stomach.

"Dad, I think I'm going to be sick," I said.

"Don't be silly," he said. "You'll be fine. Just open the window a crack and let in some fresh air."

"No, Dad. I'm going to be sick. Stop the car, Dad. Please!"

Finally he stopped the car on the shoulder of the highway. I tried to crawl over Joan's lap, but I couldn't get out the door fast enough. Most of my barf went onto the road, but some of it got on my sister's jeans. I wished Mike and Teddy could have seen her face.

"Eew, you little creep!" she screamed. "Mom, look what he did!"

"Don't worry, honey, it'll wash out," said my mom.

"But it smells bad," said Joan. "And I'm supposed to go over to Diane's place after this." She looked over at me and said, "I can't wait until you're gone!"

"You'll live," said my dad, who had gotten out and was wiping the barf from my mouth with some tissues that had traces of lipstick on them.

"Dad, are those used tissues?" I said.

"Get back in the car or we'll be late for your flight," he said.

Just to bug them, I pretended that I was moving in slow motion.

"Get in!" they all yelled.

3

When we got to the airport, we had to make a run for it. I've heard people say "make a run for it" when they don't really mean running at all, but there we were, dodging the mobs of people, all heading for better places than Point Aconi. When we finally arrived at the counter, we were greeted with another long line.

"Oh, good," said my mom, looking at the big board, "the flight has been delayed. Thank goodness!" With that, my mom and dad leaned up against the wall. Mom sat down lightly on the edge of my big green suitcase. She took out her hankie and wiped her forehead. As she let out a sigh of relief, the suitcase exploded. And there, spread out over the floor, for everyone to see, were my underwear, the beach towel with the pink mermaid on it, and my mother.

Joan started to snicker. I put my hands over my eyes and felt a hot flush spread all over my face. I wondered how many hours it would take to get to Teddy's house if I made a run for it. Maybe I could live in his parents' station wagon.

"Well," said my dad, "at least we made it."

After they stuffed my junk back into the suitcase, we got my boarding pass and walked to the gate. My mom took out a crisp twenty-dollar bill, folded it, and stuffed it into my front pocket.

"Is this a bribe?"

"Oh, Eliot," she said. I could see her eyes were kind of runny. "I'm going to miss you."

"Then why are you sending me away?" I said under my breath.

"What's that, dear?" she asked.

"Never mind," I said.

I could see the airplane out the window. The cockpit windows looked like a pair of angry eyes. It reminded me of a nasty, silver-skinned bird. Then I saw my big green suitcase. It was on a long conveyor belt heading up into the belly of the beast.

When I was at the front of the line to board, my mom got down on one knee and said, "I love you very much, Eliot. I just know you're going to have a wonderful time. Give my love to Grandma and to Uncle Earl."

I had never met Uncle Earl, but I knew Grandmother McNeil well enough. When she visited us in Lakefield the previous Easter, she complained about everything.

"I don't like crusty bread."

"I don't like feather pillows."

"You and your sister are louder than a barrel of monkeys."

"Your basement smells like radishes left to rot."

"Eliot, you know that you're much shorter than your cousin Christopher, don't you? And he's younger than you, too."

Once, when she was sticking her nose into our hall closet, I tried to squeeze past her big butt. She moved farther into the closet – and the door, which sometimes closed all by itself, locked her in. For the rest of the visit, I didn't hear the end of it. Again and again she'd tell anybody who'd listen: "That boy shoved me into a dark closet and then he slammed the door behind me. That boy has no manners whatsoever. He runs wild in the streets, Margaret." Margaret is my mother's name. "You know that you're bringing up a little hooligan, don't you?"

Why didn't Margaret understand that her little hooligan just didn't want to go spend the entire summer with her nutty family?

While Mom gave me a hug and a big kiss, Dad told me to "enjoy the aquatic opportunities," which was a fancy way of saying there'd be nothing else to do in Point Aconi.

"Hey, Dad, it's me, Eliot," I said, "your son, the kid who failed every swimming test."

"Well, kiddo," said my dad, seeming not to hear, "you catch some big fish for me, OK?"

"Bye-bye, idiot...I mean, Eliot," said my sister.

Joan loved to swim – why weren't they sending her? I didn't say another word. I just turned and walked down the gangway that led to the airplane. I might as well have been walking a pirate's plank.

When I came to the door of the airplane, I showed my ticket to the stewardess.

"Are you by yourself, young man?" she asked.

"Yes," I said with a sigh.

"Oh, so you're on a big adventure," she said with a smile.

"Um, I guess you could call it that," I said.

When I got to my seat, I could see into the terminal from my window. Mom, Dad, and Joan were still at the gate. All three were looking out, with their hands cupped over their eyes.

When they saw me, my mom began to wave frantically. I held up my hand and gave her a single wave. After a short time, my father put his arm around my mom's shoulder and motioned for my sister to follow. They turned and

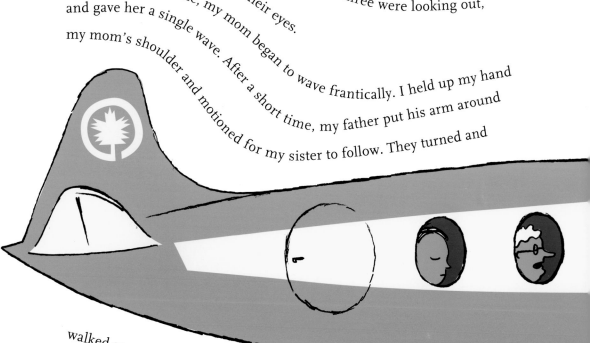

walked away. My sister looked back and stuck out her tongue.

"Welcome aboard flight 486 to Halifax, Nova Scotia," said a cheerful, nasal voice. My mother had explained that I would have to fly to Halifax first, because Point Aconi was too small to have its own airport. "As we prepare for takeoff, we invite you to review the safety features of this Vickers Viscount aircraft on the leaflet located in the seat pocket in front of you." I buckled my seat belt and waited.

Finally, the engines screamed and everything began to shake. As we took off, I held onto the armrests to stop from getting sucked back into my seat.

My ears popped a few times, but as soon as the plane was in the air, everything quieted down a bit. The drone of the engines made me sleepy. The stewardess came back and gave me some water, a little bag of peanuts, and a tiny toy replica of the airplane we were in.

"Have you ever been to Nova Scotia?" she asked.

"No," I said.

"You're going to love it," she said.

"Are you working for my mother?"

The stewardess just laughed. I took that as a yes.

After she left, I fell asleep and dreamed that Teddy and Mike were grown-ups with beards. They were sitting in a tent reading Spider-man comics, but they were so tall their heads brushed the ceiling of the tent. Mike was saying, "I wonder whatever happened to Eliot?"

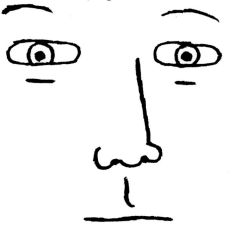

"Who knows?" said Teddy, twirling his beard. "I don't even remember why we were ever friends with that little kid."

Then Mike said, "We are on our final approach into Halifax Airport. Please restore your seats to the upright position, fasten your seat belts, and ensure that your tray tables are locked."

When I got off the plane in Halifax, an icy wind made me shiver. I could even see my breath. Perfect! I'd been waiting forever for summer to come and my parents had shipped me to Siberia.

We were marched across the tarmac and into a room with a luggage carousel. The machine kept going around and around, but my suitcase never showed up. Soon, I was the only person staring at the square hole in the wall where the bags came out, hoping to see the one thing I had left to remind me of home.

A big man with blue dungarees and a flat face squeezed in through a little yellow door beside the turnstile and said, "Hey, kid, is this here suitcase yours?"

"I think so," I said. It looked like my suitcase, but there was yellow tape wrapped around it.

"She busted open in cargo," he said, "so we had to close 'er up."

Great, I thought, I wouldn't want to fly all the way to Nova Scotia without first making sure the people here had the chance to inspect my underwear.

I thanked him and grabbed the suitcase. It was heavy, so I had to drag it to the exit. Just then, a long, shiny, gold car pulled up. The woman in the driver's seat was leaning forward – almost hugging the steering wheel. Her long, thin nose was pointed high into the air so that it didn't bump into the wheel. It was Grandmother McNeil. I'd recognize that nose anywhere.

"I'm taking you straight to Point Aconi," said Grandmother McNeil. "I hope you went pee at the airport because there'll be no stops along the way – I'll be dropping you two off, and then I've got a golf game this afternoon."

"You two" meant me and her brother, my great-uncle, Earl, who got out of the car to help me with my suitcase. He was a lanky old man in a dark green work shirt, with big black boots on his feet. One of his sleeves was rolled up, revealing a leathery arm with a faded anchor tattoo.

A gold tooth in his creased mouth glinted in the sun. I came up to about his elbow. He seemed to be studying me – getting an eyeful, as my mother would say. I looked down, but I could still feel his icy stare. I shivered as it sank in that this strange pirate of a man would be my jailer for the entire summer. "You're pretty small for twelve, huh?" he said.

"Gee, I've never heard that before," I said, climbing into the back seat. Grandmother McNeil pulled out onto the road at the speed of an inchworm. I hadn't had to pee before she mentioned it, but now I started squirming.

"Listen up, boy," she said to me. "Let me tell you a few things about Point Aconi. There's more going on there than meets the eye."

"Oh, good!" I said, and I meant it. I really wanted to be wrong. I was hoping she'd tell me about a visiting circus with elephants and baboons, or a nearby summer camp where I'd make so many friends that Mike and Teddy would be jealous.

"Number one," she said, "you'll be eating the best shellfish you've ever tried, and your uncle's the one who'll teach you how to catch your dinner."

Uncle Earl turned around and gave me another long look. His face was heavily lined, and his scalp was covered in thick, spiky gray hair. He seemed to be trying to figure out whether to keep me or throw me back.

"Number two," she started and then turned into a lane of oncoming traffic. Horns started honking. One driver stuck his hand out the window as Grandmother McNeil swerved back into her lane. "Sunday drivers!" she yelled.

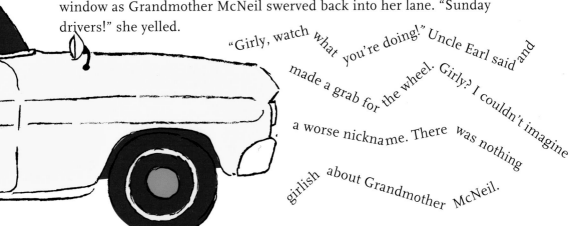

"Girly, watch what you're doing!" Uncle Earl said and made a grab for the wheel. Girly? I couldn't imagine a worse nickname. There was nothing girlish about Grandmother McNeil.

"I was just merging!" she insisted. "Now, as I was saying, the number three thing you need to know is –"

"What happened to number two?" I interrupted.

"Don't talk back to your elders, Eliot. Hasn't your mother taught you a thing? Number three: Did you know that Point Aconi sits on top of one of the biggest coal seams in Nova Scotia?" The way she asked the question made me think that I was supposed to be impressed, but I didn't even know what a coal seam was.

"Um," I said.

"Well, it does," she said. "And it's worth a king's ransom too."

"To some," Earl chimed in.

"To the Bushwhacker Coal Company for one," Grandmother McNeil said. "I know the money-grubbing snake who owns that company – Billy Bush," she said with a sigh. "I almost married him, but that was a long time ago. If I did marry him, I'd be a whole lot richer, and you wouldn't be here today, Eliot." That sounded just fine to me. I perked up.

"It's all politics," Earl said, staring out the window. He seemed to be a man of few words, and that was fine by me. After that, the conversation trailed off for a bit. It took forever to get to the turnoff. Point Aconi Road snaked along the edge of a reddish-brown river. On the way, we passed lots of little houses, a wharf with colorful fishing boats that jutted out into the river, a little variety store called What's the Point, and an ancient, overgrown cemetery. When the car got to the top of the hill, I was looking at the ocean for the first time. I looked out to where it met the sky – other than the sky, it was the biggest thing I'd ever seen.

Grandmother McNeil looked at me in the rearview mirror and raised one of her eyebrows. She picked up where she left off. "All I'm saying is that I've been trying to get Earl to sell that place to Bushwhacker for years. We could get a pretty penny for it. Legally that place is half mine anyway. He could give up fishing altogether and move into town with civilized folk. After all, fishing is a tough life, and he's not getting any younger."

"I can hear you, Girly, and I'm not giving up fishing. What would I do, sit around and watch TV all day?"

"No, you could go for walks and visit friends."

"The walkin' is just as good in Point Aconi as any other place. And anyhow, all my friends are here."

"You could make new friends."

"Enough, Girly."

"You'll see for yourself, Eliot, what kind of a place Point Aconi is. Maybe by the time you're through with us, you'll be able to convince your uncle to move to greener pastures – somewhere nice like Sydney, or even Lakefield."

I was trying to follow their conversation, but more than anything I was desperate to pee, and I was relieved when we finally turned into what looked like a driveway. I caught a quick glimpse of a small black-and-white house and a faded light blue pickup truck standing by a large unpainted barn shed.

Hanging on a clothesline, waving in the breeze, was a neat row of what looked to be dried fish.

I practically leaped out of the car. A scruffy dog came barreling towards me and immediately started to sniff my shoes.

"Meet Happy," Earl said.

"I have to pee really badly."

Uncle Earl grimaced and gestured that I should go around to the back of the barn to the field. The joy of my relief was interrupted by the sound of bickering, but I couldn't make out what Grandmother McNeil and Earl were saying.

By the time I walked back, Grandmother was gone. "Will we be seeing...a lot of her?" I asked Uncle Earl.

"Hopefully not," Earl said, and that was one thing we could agree upon.

5

"C'mon, kid, I'll take you to your room and show you around the place."

We climbed up the steps to the back porch, which was littered with fishing gear. Beside the entrance, there was a row of slickers with matching rain hats hanging on hooks. Under the slickers was a row of Wellington boots – some black, some green, some large, some small.

"I've got a pair of wellies and a slicker that just might fit you," Earl said, pointing at the boots and coats.

The freaky idea that I was actually going to be fishing with this man out in the middle of the ocean seemed more real.

"Did my mom mention that I'm not a very good swimmer?" I asked.

He mumbled something I couldn't make out and continued with the tour. "Through here is the kitchen. I hope you're not a fussy eater. I'm not much of a cook, so don't expect me to make whatever it is you eat in Lakefield."

"Stale bread and water?"

"What's that?"

"Nothing."

"And through here are the bedrooms and the washroom," he went on, motioning with his head. We walked into a narrow hallway with four closed doors. He tilted his head to the right and said, "I'm giving you Girly's old room."

The musty-smelling room had a large brass bed in the center. The fringed bedcover was a faded pink color with rows of little white and brown balls. On the wall above the bed hung a yellowed photograph of a stern-looking lady with a brimmed sun hat. "That's your great-grandmother, Minnie Purvis," said Earl.

Her piercing eyes followed me as I made my way around to the end of the bed. She seemed to say...

Earl bent down to put my suitcase on the floor but let it drop when a stab of pain made him wince. "Bad back. Come outside when you're finished putting your stuff away," he said between clenched teeth.

Everything in that room was old and girlish – even the lampshade was decorated with pink flowers. I looked up again at the faded photograph of Great-grandmother Purvis. She looked back down – "I'm watching you, boy. I'm watching you."

I lifted the twisted mess of clothes from my suitcase and put them away in the dresser. I put the two books my mother had packed – *The Invisible Man* by H.G. Wells, and *Never Cry Wolf* by Farley Mowat – on the bedstand and shoved the mermaid towel under the chest of drawers.

When I came back out onto the driveway, Earl and Happy were sitting on the porch. I looked down the drive and saw a girl about my age, with three little kids in tow, walking towards us. "The word is out," said Earl. "I told a few of the neighborhood kids that you were coming to stay for the summer. They must have seen Girly's Pontiac."

As she came closer I said, "Hi, I'm Eliot."

Hi, I'm Mary Beth. These three runts here are my brothers, Tim, Mick, and Frankie. I hafta look after them," she said with a sigh.

"Don't, Mary Breath."

"Who you?"

"Flub."

The three little kids came up to about her waist. They were all roughly the same age and had the same ragged, dirty white T-shirts and shorts. All four kids – Mary Beth included – were in bare feet. She had big brown eyes and long chestnut hair. She was wearing a whitish dress that looked like it had been washed too many times, but she was pretty in a way that I never thought pretty could be. More hard than soft. More angular than round.

"Mary Beth's dad helps out on my boat," said Earl. "You'll meet him tomorrow morning – that is, if I can get you out of bed early enough."

"Already?" I protested. "It'll be my first day of vacation!"

Mary Beth gave me a long, hard look. She stared at my shoes and slowly worked her way up to my face. "Can he come swimming with us?" she asked Earl, who was taking a long breath before he answered me.

Earl let out his breath. He seemed relieved. "Yes! Take him, and take Happy with you, and be back in two hours for dinner."

Happy, who seemed to understand a lot more than I did, jumped from the steps and came brushing up against my leg. I bent down to pat him, and he licked me on the nose.

"I'll take these here monsters home and be back for you," said Mary Beth. She headed away with her brothers in tow.

I ran into the bedroom, wiggled open my drawer, and took out my blue bathing suit. I looked down at the mermaid towel sticking out from the bottom of the chest of drawers, closed my eyes, and grabbed it. As I left the room, I caught a glimpse of Great-grandmother Purvis. "What's your problem?" I asked the photograph. "I'm just going swimming."

When Mary Beth finally came back, she looped her arm through mine and spun us around. "This way," she said as she pulled me along. I felt a hot flash, and I knew my face was turning red, but I wished that Mike and Teddy could see me now.

"So, yer from Lakefield, I hear," she said as we crossed the road.

"Yes," I said. "And you're from Point Aconi?"

She snorted a laugh. "Never been gone from it...Eliot, is it?"

"Um, yes, Eliot Dionisi," I said.

"Dionisi? What kind of name is that?"

"Um, it's an Italian name – my father is Italian. Well, he can't speak it, but his parents were Italian."

"We're the McGilliverys," she said. "How old are you, Eliot?"

"I'm twelve and a half," I said.

"Ha, I'm thirteen," she said. "Well, I just turned thirteen.

Anyways, look, here are the others."

"Others?" I asked.

"That's Jack and Eddie
McLeod," she said, pointing
at two look-alike boys with
sandy hair who came plowing
through the tall grass. "Jack
and Eddie are good boys, but

you've got to watch out for their older brother, Donnie. He has a
mean streak, and he won't like some Eye-talian kid from away coming
around." Following behind the McLeod brothers was another boy –
a skinny kid with blond curls. "And that's Timmy Jenkins," she said,
pointing with her chin. She was shaking her head. "Well, everybody
loves Timmy, but he's a bit slow in the head, if you know what I mean.
Donnie is probably hardest on poor old Timmy."

Poor old Timmy? What about me? The words "he won't like some
Eye-talian kid from away" were still ringing in my ears.

"Hallo, Mary Beth," said the taller of the sandy-haired boys.
"Well, what have we got here?"

"Jack, this here is Eliot Dionisi," said Mary Beth. "He's sort of
an Eye-talian or some such." All three boys had towels rolled up
under their arms.

"Eye-talian, eh," said Eddie. "Donnie's not going to like that."

"I already told him," said Mary Beth.

"Well, never mind about that now," said Eddie, the younger
McLeod boy. "It's getting hot, so let's go swimming at the Sandy Spot."

We started down a path that cut through a blueberry patch.
Happy scampered ahead. Then we passed through a field of shrubs
and prickly brambles and entered a stand of evergreens. To the
right was a large pond with dark amber water.

"Don't ever go swimming in that muck," said Jack. "That's left
over from the coal mines, and swimming in it will poison you. Least
that's what my pa says."

When we broke through the evergreens, I could see the ocean.

It was grayish green, more the color of split pea soup than of a swimming pool.

We passed through a tiny graveyard with twenty or so stone markers.

"I'll be right back," said Mary Beth as she ducked under a tree and entered the graveyard. The rest of us walked on and came to the top of a ridge. "And this," said Jack, looking down, "is the Sandy Spot." At the bottom of a half circle of giant gray rocks was a tiny crescent-shaped patch of brown beach. When we got to the rocks, all three boys peeled down to their bathing trunks.

"Um, are there any changing rooms?" I asked.

They laughed out loud. "Changing rooms!" repeated Timmy. "Where do you think we are, the French Ravioli?"

"You can change behind one of the stones back in the graveyard," said Jack, "but be careful, I think that's what Mary Beth is doing."

That's just perfect, I thought, they use graveyards for changing rooms in Point Aconi. I climbed back up and whispered loudly,

"Mary Beth...are you there?"

She didn't answer so I found a marker to hide behind. I stripped off my clothes and had another pee. Then I pulled up my trunks and, like I had seen the other boys do, rolled my clothes into my towel. I walked around to the front of the marker and read the name:

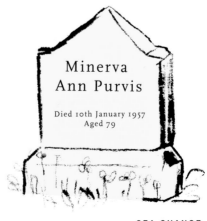

Minerva
Ann Purvis

Died 10th January 1957
Aged 79

Oh, no! I had just peed on my great-grandmother's gravestone. Her face in the yellowed photograph came back. "I'm watching you, boy. I'm watching you."

I scrambled down to the beach and dropped my bundle.

"C'mon in, the water's fine," said Eddie. I went in up to my ankles.

"It's awfully cold," I said.

"You'll get used to it," said Jack. They were far in, splashing each other and yelling happily. Then Mary Beth appeared and called out from the top of the rocks. "How's the water?" she asked.

I quickly waded out to my waist. "It's f-fine," I said.

She climbed down the rocks and waded in. "Fine? It's friggin' freezing," she said. But then she dove in and joined the others.

Perfect, my new "friends" were all semi-professional swimmers. What a great match this was.

Fortunately, they didn't stay long and they didn't seem to notice or care that I didn't come out any farther. We all spread out our

towels on the flat rocks.

"That's a beautiful towel," said Mary Beth.

"Are you serious?" I asked. "I'm not a big fan of pink. Or mermaids."

"It's a lot nicer than mine," she said, pointing to her small white towel. I looked more closely and saw that it had frayed edges, and I felt kind of bad for complaining about a stupid towel.

closed I looked around and saw that all the kids had their eyes, so I closed mine too. After a while, I opened my right eye a crack and looked around. These kids seemed so confident and relaxed. So easy to make friends with. Maybe the summer was going to have some OK moments after all.

When the sun was just hitting the water, Timmy said, "We'd buh-better hightail it. The buh-black flies will bah-be out any second, and they'll eat us alive." He spoke slowly and stuttered, but nobody laughed or made fun of him. Then I remembered what Mary Beth said about Timmy being slow.

We bundled up our things and walked back along the path. When we arrived back at the blueberry patch, the path split off in two directions.

"This is us," said Jack. "Me and Eddie are workin' on Pa's boat for the summer, so we'll see ya at the wharf tomorrow morning, Eliot."

I was about to tell them that kids in Lakefield didn't work when they were on vacation, but I saw that everyone, especially Mary Beth, was watching me closely.

"OK," I said.

"Bye!" said Timmy, waving at me happily. The three boys headed left while Mary Beth and I headed right.

Night was falling, but Happy, who kept looking back impatiently, led the way to Earl's. "That's one of the smartest dogs I ever seen," said Mary Beth.

I looked around and noticed that it was already getting dark. Then I looked up. "We don't have this many stars in Lakefield," I said.

"I guess that's one thing we got here," she said. "You must find us a little –"

Earl's voice, calling from one of the windows, interrupted. "Is that you, Eliot boy?"

"Yes, sir!" I answered.

"Get in here for dinner," he said. "We have an early start tomorrow."

Even in the half-light, I could sense that Mary Beth was studying me. "See you tomorrow, Eliot Dionisi," said Mary Beth as she disappeared down the driveway.

I stood there for a little bit longer, looking at the spot where she had disappeared. Was it possible that a girl like Mary Beth could like a boy like me? The other boys seemed a lot like her – strong and easygoing. Well, not Timmy, he was more like me, shy and awkward. Maybe she was just being nice and didn't really like me in the girlfriend-boyfriend way. After all, she was nice to Timmy too. Maybe it was all in my head. Then I heard the sputter and sizzle of something frying in the kitchen, and it smelled pretty good.

"I hope you like tongue and onions," said Earl. On the stove, in a big black cast-iron skillet, was a pink cow's tongue. The top had the same surface as my own tongue, and at the thick end, I could see all the veins and muscles that were once attached to the cow.

I gagged and almost threw up.

"No, I...I'm allergic to tongues," I blurted, while rubbing the roof of my mouth with my own.

"Allergic, eh?" he asked. "How about pickled pigs' feet? I have a fresh jar in the fridge. I also have a big container of head cheese if that suits your fancy." I didn't know or want to know what head cheese was.

Happy came in licking his chops and then sat with his head tucked under Earl's chair.

I summoned all my courage.

"Um, like, do you have, like, grilled cheese or something like that?" I asked.

"Boy, if you're going to survive in Point Aconi, you'll have to learn to eat real food."

And who told him I wanted to survive? I'd rather die than eat tongues and feet and heads.

But in the meantime I was hungry and grateful when I saw Earl pull down another skillet from a hook on the wall. He stuck a butter knife into a tub of margarine and scraped a dollop off onto the inside edge of the pan. "Get me two pieces of bread from the freezer and a slice of cheese from the door in the fridge."

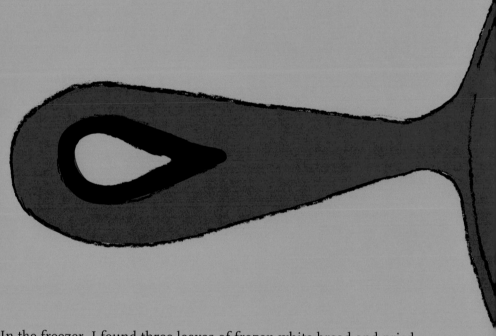

In the freezer, I found three loaves of frozen white bread and pried two slices out from one of them. In the fridge, there was a jar filled with gray-colored pigs' feet on the top shelf. I suppressed another gag and found the packet of cheese slices in one of the door compartments.

I handed Earl the three items, and he dropped one of the frozen slices into the sizzling margarine. Then he put the cheese slice on top and capped it off with the second piece of bread.

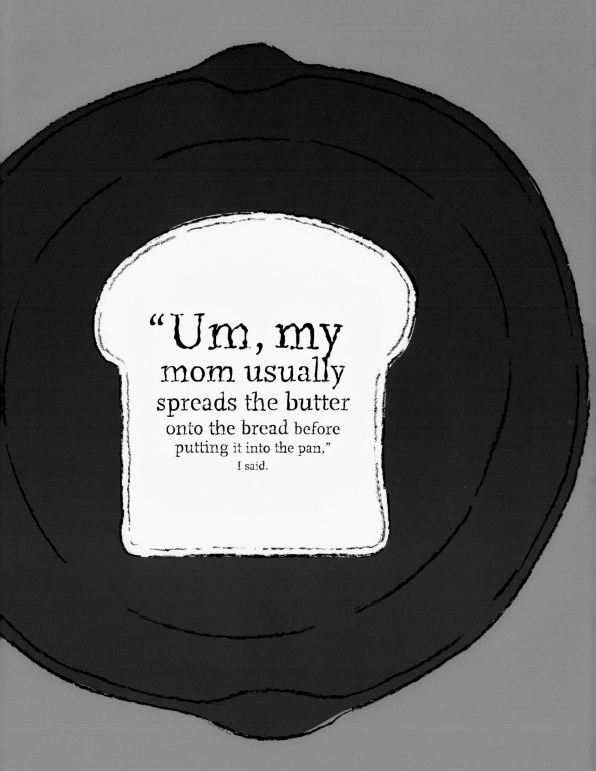

"Um, my mom usually spreads the butter onto the bread before putting it into the pan," I said.

"Your mother is a smart lady," said Earl, "but this here is the way we make a grilled cheese in Point Aconi."

There was a pause as I considered my options.

"Do you have ketchup?" I asked.

"No, boy."

I sat down as Earl slid the grilled cheese onto my plate. It looked like a slab of plywood. He didn't even remove the crust or cut it into two diagonal pieces, like my mom always did.

He poured the tea into two fancy cups that were chipped and stained.

He had brewed a pot of tea. "Milk and sugar?"

"Yes, please," I said.

Then he poured two heaping spoonfuls of sugar and lots of canned evaporated milk into each cup. I took a sip of the hot tea. It was sweet, but the milk tasted funny.

"Eat," he said as he carved a slice of tongue from his plate. He speared the wedge of gray meat with his fork and used his knife to top it off with a pile of fried onions. As he lifted the disgusting pile to his mouth, I closed my eyes and took a tiny bite of the grilled cheese. It was tasteless. I chewed slowly, swallowed, and took another tiny bite.

My thoughts must have been written on my face. "Chin up, kid, we'll have something special tomorrow night," he said with a grin.

Something special? Now that sounded scary.

The next morning arrived in the middle of the night with a rapping
at my bedroom door.

"Get up, kid. The day's a wastin'."

I opened one eye and thought about playing dead – whenever
I played dead at home, my mom would tickle me until I couldn't
stand it anymore. But I didn't want to risk the same treatment
from my uncle.

"Yes, sir," I said loudly enough for him to hear.

I stretched for a minute or so and then threw the covers from
the bed. When my feet hit the linoleum floor, it was like an ice rink.
A million goose bumps ran up and down my legs. The air was so cold
I could see my breath as I traded my pajamas for a sweater and pants.

I stumbled out into the kitchen, where Earl was frying back
bacon and home fries. He pointed over to the toaster and said, "Pop
that toast, butter 'em up, and put two more pieces in 'er. How do
you like your eggs?"

"Um, scrambled, sir." It was a big breakfast and a big improvement over the grilled cheese, but the milk tasted funny, and there was no ketchup for my eggs.

"I packed us ham sandwiches and apples for lunch. You do eat ham, don't you?"

When we got to the hall, Earl pointed to a pair of green Wellington boots. "Those might fit you. And put on these dungarees and that little slicker," he said, indicating a big yellow coat that looked like it was made from rubber. I climbed into the dungarees, but they were way too long.

"Don't just stand there, kid – roll 'em up." He looked me up and down and grimaced like he had never seen anything so pathetic.

As we left the porch and headed for the pickup, it was still pitch black outside. "What time is it?" I asked.

"Five thirty-five," he said, looking down at his watch. "We're running late." Running late? I'd never been up this early in my whole life.

Earl threw two coils of thick rope into the back of the pickup. I got a sense he was ready to handle me the same way.

"Climb in," he said. Happy jumped in before me and took the middle spot.

The beams of Earl's headlights lit up a thick blanket of low-lying fog on the winding road. We came out of the fog at the top of every hill and descended back in at the bottom.

"How can you see the road?" I asked, praying he was a better driver than Grandmother McNeil.

"I know it like the back of my hand," said Earl, but every few seconds we'd hit the gravel on the edge and Earl would have to jerk the truck back onto the road.

I could see the headlines in the Lakefield newspaper:

The Lakefield

Special
Edition

EXAMINER 10¢

LOCAL BOY ELIOT DIONISI DIES IN TRUCK WRECK WITH MANGY DOG AND CRANKY OLD MAN

Last known photograph of Eliot Dionisi.

The city of Lakefield is in a state of shock as it attempts to cope with the loss of one of its finest citizens. Letters of condolence are pouring in from as far away as Woodville. "We're going to miss him," said one letter.

PARENTS QUESTIONED
Why did they send him?

Police are questioning Mr. and Mrs. Dionisi about the loss of their son, Eliot. Among other things, they want to know why the couple sent their only son to a remote part of the country so soon after finishing his school year. "I mean, it just doesn't add up," said police chief Andrews. "The kid had been waiting the entire year to spend the summer with his friends in Lakefield, and then whoosh, just like that, they sent him off to Point Aconi. Even the name of the place sounds dangerous."

Lakefield Weeps Over Loss of Last True Son

"He was here and then he was gone," said one anonymous attendee at Eliot Dionisi's funeral. "He was Lakefield's last true son," said another onlooker who asked not to be identified. All agreed that he was cut down – under extremely suspicious circumstances – in the very prime of his short life.

Mike and Teddy Claim Ownership of Eliot's Comic Book Collection

Mike and Teddy, neighbors of the dead boy, claim that Eliot told them before he left for Point Aconi that if anything should happen to him, they could have his comic book collection. "There are several rare, important specimens in the collection and we want to make sure they end up in the right hands," said police chief Andrews.

Sister Joan Moves into Brother's Bedroom While Body Still Warm

According to one source, Joan Dionisi, sister of the slain boy, moved into her brother's bedroom only days after his death. Joan's ex-boyfriend Harold added, "She didn't even wait until his coffin was in the ground." Rumors persist that Eliot's guitar was listed for sale in a local paper.

"A Sad Day" Says Mayor Ford

"The loss of...what's the boy's name again? Oh yes, Eliot. The loss of Eliot marks a sad day for Lakefield," said Mayor Ford. "I will make it my life's work to catch the perpetrators," he later added.

MATH TEACHER CLAIMS THAT ELIOT IS STILL ALIVE IN PARALLEL DIMENSION

Mr. Able, Eliot's math teacher at Lakefield Junior High, claims that Eliot came to him in a dream and told him that he was fine and living in a parallel dimension. "There's a Lakefield here too," said Eliot. "Don't worry about me. I like it here because I don't have a sister and my parents are much nicer."

"He also told me that they don't have potato chips in that dimension so I'm working on a machine to send a bag or two across the void," added Mr. Able.

Finally, we reached the wharf, which was lit by two large yellow lights atop wooden posts. It was L-shaped and had about twenty fishing boats tied to either side.

There were about the same number of tiny wooden shacks near the entrance to the dock – some brightly painted and others weathered and in bad repair. Earl pulled a key from his slicker and opened the padlock of a tidy-looking one, painted white with black trim. A horrible smell greeted us as he opened the door. I gagged and threw up a little into my mouth.

"That's our bait shack," Earl said as he waved me over to the entrance. "Time to get to work."

There was a wooden trough at the back filled with half-rotten fish. Thousands of white maggots were moving in and around the decomposed chunks.

Earl chuckled and said, "That's rotting mackerel, boy – lobsters are bottom feeders, and they love it – the smellier the better. I'm going to take a few supplies down to the boat while you fill those buckets with bait. Use the pitchfork, boy. And hop to it!"

Against the right wall was a worn pitchfork, and on the left were three large white buckets with metal handles. I pulled the neck of my sweater over my nose and held my breath, but when I lifted the pitchfork, the sweater slipped back down. I breathed in, gagged, and ran for the exit.

I wondered if Earl had left the keys in his truck, but then I remembered that I didn't know how to drive. With no escape in sight, I figured it was better to hurry before I died of fish fumes, so I rushed back in.

I shoved the pitchfork into the mess and scraped off the first load into one of the buckets. I had to take several breaks, but I finally managed to fill all three buckets with the disgusting stuff.

I spun around as I caught sight of something moving from the corner of my eye. Standing half in shadow in the doorway was a short, pear-shaped man. He was wearing a slicker, but his big belly kept it from closing at the front. It was a little too long in the arms so all I could see were the tips of his sausage-like fingers. He had a big red nose and a tuft of wavy black hair on the top of his fat head.

"So you're Eliot, eh?" he said.

"Yes, sir," I answered.

"You know my daughter, Mary Beth," he said. He was chewing something big and talked like he had marbles in his mouth.

"Yes, sir," I answered. "I met her yesterday."

"Is that right now? She told me you was swimmin' with her at the Sandy Spot, no?" he asked.

"Yes, sir."

After a long silence, he added, "I know my Mary Beth, and I think she took a fancy to you, Eliot boy. So listen close now, if you wanna stay healthy, you keep your place around my Mary Beth, all right then?"

"Yessir, all right," I answered. I was glad to hear he thought Mary Beth liked me, but I also knew that dads didn't always under-stand their kids. And anyway, what did he mean "keep your place"?

"Good. Me name is Dermot, but you can call me Mister McGillivery." Then he rolled something around inside his cheek.

With that, he spat out a big yellow wad of chewing tobacco.

It landed right beside my boot. I looked down at it, expecting to see a tangle of squirming maggots.

"Here now, I'll take two buckets down to the boat and you take de udder one." He motioned towards one of the buckets with a tilt of his fat head.

Earl's boat, the YNOT, was smaller than some of the other boats, but it was clean and tidy. I climbed slowly down the wooden ladder and stepped carefully onto the deck. There was lots of activity on the other boats – men stacking traps, orders being barked, and engines starting up with a deep, bubbly growl. Through the mist, I could see Jack and Eddie McLeod working on a red-and-white boat. I waved, but they didn't see me.

"Eliot, climb up top and cast off the ropes," Earl instructed.

"Who, me?" I asked.

"Up, boy!" he said. I crept back up and looked down.

"Untie the ropes," barked Earl. "Pull the end through the first loop, and then just pull it hard." When I couldn't get it, Earl sighed and whispered something under his breath. Mister McGillivery climbed up and snatched the rope from my hand. He had both ropes untied in a few seconds.

"Get aboard," said Earl as he took his spot in the wheelhouse. He cranked the engine a few times. It whined and complained miserably before it finally roared awake. I was following Mister McGillivery down the ladder and just managed to get back onto the YNOT before she pulled away.

Why didn't I just stay in bed and pretend to be dead? He might've believed it. Even being tickled by Uncle Earl wouldn't have been so bad compared to this.

Earl spun the wheel and pointed the YNOT towards the open ocean. As we picked up speed, a hint of deep orange appeared on the horizon.

"It'll take a good forty-five minutes before we reach the traps, so make yourself comfortable," said Earl as he wiped the dew from the wheelhouse windows with his sleeve. I was starting to get the familiar sick feeling in the pit of my stomach.

"Can I look down over the front deck?" I asked.

"Suit yourself," said Earl.

I carefully worked my way along the side of the wheelhouse and pulled myself up onto the bow. I held tightly onto the cleats and lay down on my stomach with my head looking over the bow. Happy joined me. The surface of the water was dead calm in this moving window of momentary space before the *YNOT* cut through it.

Looking through the green depths, I could see the rocky bottom. I caught a glimpse of a diamond-shaped skate fish combing the rocks. Farther on, I thought I saw the skeleton of a sunken lobster boat.

The surface became rougher, and my window on the ocean floor gradually disappeared. I crawled back and joined Earl in the wheelhouse. "Why did you call her the *YNOT*?" I asked.

"Why not?" he answered. I figured he'd used that line more than a few times. "OK, what's your middle name?" he asked.

"Anthony," I said with a groan. I hated that name and didn't tell anybody at my school back in Lakefield.

"Right, and what's *YNOT* backwards?" he asked.

"TONY," I said. I looked up at him suspiciously.

"Right, and what's Tony short for?"

"Anthony," I said slowly. "You mean the *YNOT* is named after me?" I couldn't believe it: they all started planning for me to be here, on this boat, before I was even born? Maybe my whole life had already been planned. Maybe I'd never get to do anything I liked ever again. I looked over at Earl. When he registered the look of horror on my face, his expression changed from a gentle smirk to anger.

"Named after you?" he said. "I took delivery of her around the time you were born. I named her after the son of my favorite niece. I didn't know you at the time." I could hear the sarcasm in his voice.

Yeah, I thought, and you still don't know me, you freaky old man.

"Get back up front," he said. "I have work to do."

On the bright side, if the boat sank, my last resting place would have my name on it, even if it was only my crappy middle name spelled backwards.

"There's our first trap, Dermot," shouted Earl, idling the engine. "Grab the gaff." Mister McGillivery caught the buoy with the gaff – a tool with a long wooden handle and a big hook at the end. Happy started barking.

By this time, the fog was all but gone, and the surface of the water reflected the color of the overcast sky – a ghostly gray. McGillivery pulled in the wooden buoy and let it drop with a thud onto the deck. He wound a coil of the rope around a large metal spool and pulled a lever. With a whine of groaning gears, the wheel began to turn, adding another coil of rope to the spool with each rotation. I leaned over the edge, hoping to catch a glimpse of the trap before it reached the surface.

"How deep is the water?" I asked Earl.

"Right here? About thirty fathoms," he answered.

"What's a fathom?" I asked.

"Don't they have schools in Lakefield?" he growled. "I'm about one fathom tall." I tried to imagine thirty Earls stacked one on top of the other. And that, I thought, was thirty Earls too many.

"Your job, boy, is to band the claws with these," he said, pointing to an old coffee tin filled with thick blue rubber bands. "That way, when you put the lobsters in the bin," he said pointing to a large wooden crate behind the engine compartment, "they won't harm each other and they'll be easier to handle when we weigh in at the government dock." There was just one lobster in the first trap. It was greenish brown and looked exactly like a monster from a horror movie.

Mister McGillivery reached in and handed it to Earl. "Let me show you, boy: with your left hand, hold it here behind the head so it can't pinch you with its claws. Grab a rubber band, hold the claw shut and slip one of the bands over it. Then do the same with the smaller claw. After that, put it gently in the crate and you're done until the next trap. Got it?"

"I think so," I said. I was secretly wishing they wouldn't catch any more of those things.

Mister McGillivery let go a snort and said, "You'd better have got it b'ye, or you'll be losing a pinky or two." To add emphasis, he leaned over the edge of the boat, squeezed his two nostrils, and pulled down with a snort. A large wad of green snot shot out and into the water. Happy stood up on his hind legs with his front paws cupped over the gunwale to have a look at the floating green goo.

If Mister McGillivery lived in the ocean, I thought, he'd be a bottom feeder for sure.

Then he grabbed a glove full of rotting bait from one of the buckets and shoved it into the trap. He dropped the trap back overboard and let the rope slide lightly through his gloves until it was all the way back on the bottom of the ocean floor. He threw the buoy back out hard enough to clear the YNOT's propeller. Earl pushed down on the throttle, spun the wheel, and headed in the direction of the next buoy.

The traps were set in a straight line. The distance between each buoy was arranged so that they were as far away from each other as possible, but not so far that you wouldn't be able to see the next one.

At the next trap, Mister McGillivery handed me my first lobster, but I dropped it on the deck. He screamed and grabbed me by the arm.

He squeezed me so hard, I yelped in pain.

"Dermot," said Earl, "let go of the boy. What do you think you're doing?"

"Aw, I didn't hurt him," he said, but my arm was aching. At the next trap, I dropped a lobster overboard, and Mister McGillivery growled and looked over at Earl.

"Take a break, kid," said Earl.

I made my way up to the bow and sat on the little bench as Earl and Mister McGillivery continued working. Over the edge I could see a distant shoreline with gently rolling green hills. If only I'd made more of an effort at swimming class.

When they had finished two lines of traps, Earl shut down the engine and brought out lunch. He handed me a sandwich and poured a cup of sweet milky tea from a thermos. I took a sip and sort of liked it this time. Maybe I was getting used to the food. Then again, maybe I was just hungry.

"You can try again tomorrow, boy," said Earl. "With any luck, before the end of the season, you'll be hauling and baiting traps yourself." As I rubbed my aching arm, I thought that with any luck I'd be out of this lunatic asylum long before that ever happened.

By the time they finished the third and final line, the wooden crate was filled to the top with lobsters. The last task was to bring in a very long fishing line that Earl had marked with a different series of black-and-white buoys. There were large hooks on the line – spaced out every four feet or so.

On most hooks they had caught mackerel, but on othe

Whatever they caught, they whacked it on the head, chopped it up, and threw it into one of the buckets. They re-baited each hook with a small piece of fresh fish and let the line back out – hook by hook by hook. When they were finished, we were heading back to the wharf with three buckets of fresh bait and a full load of lobster.

By this time, the sky was a bright turquoise blue that reflected back onto the surface of the choppy sea. It was getting warm, so I took off my slicker. Using it as a pillow, I lay down on the deck beside the bench. Happy lay down beside me with his head resting on my stomach. I think he felt bad for me. Before I drifted off to sleep, I looked up and saw Earl looking down at me. His face was framed in the wheelhouse window. He was a dead ringer for his mother with that same "I'm watching you, boy" look on his face. If they didn't like what they saw, they could just send me straight back to Lakefield. Mike and Teddy would agree that the only sane thing to do with a live lobster was to drop it.

When we arrived at the Point Aconi wharf around two thirty, Mary Beth and Timmy were waiting.

"Good catch?" Mary Beth yelled down to her father.

"A full-up crate," said Mister McGillivery.

She turned in my direction. "Jack and Eddie are just finishing up some chores. They'll be along. Come swimmin' with us, Eliot?"

I looked over at Earl, who said, "Go, we've got a good half hour's work here. Be ready to leave."

"But I don't have my bathing suit or towel," I answered.

they caught stranger-looking fish like skates and rockfish. They even caught a dogfish, a kind of small shark

"Then swim in your pants, boy. And you don't need a towel on a day like this."

"We'll walk him home, Mister Purvis," said Mary Beth.

"Even better!" said Earl. "Happy, you stay with Eliot," he added as he helped the old dog up the ladder to the wharf.

We walked over to a place where there were no boats parked and joined up with Jack and Eddie. Jack was the first to dive in. His arc through the air was graceful, and he hardly made a splash when he hit the water. He was followed in quick succession by Mary Beth, Eddie, and Timmy.

"C'mon in, Eliot!" yelled Jack. I looked down. It was a good twelve feet from the top of the wharf to the water. I had never dived that far. I'd never even jumped that far. I didn't want the gang to think I was a baby, but I knew I couldn't do it. Besides, my arm was still aching.

"I'll take the ladder down," I said as I pulled off my dungarees, boots, sweater, and T-shirt. "My mom said never to dive if you don't know how deep the water is."

"It's a good two fathoms deep," said Mary Beth.

Hmm, two Earls deep I thought, but I pretended not to hear her.

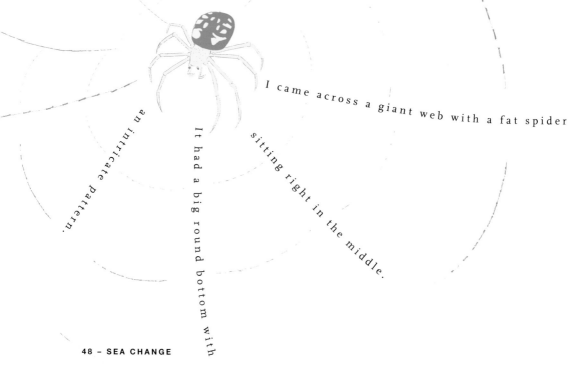

I came across a giant web with a fat spider sitting right in the middle. It had a big round bottom with an intricate pattern.

This was too much – I screeched and jumped into the water. By the time I popped back up to the surface, the shock of the ice-cold water was making my teeth chatter. I shivered and began to dog paddle in a circle. Mary Beth swam up and said, "Are you all right, Eliot?"

"It's cold," I said.

"You'll get used to it," she said with a laugh. "C'mon, we're swimming over to the *Miss Louisa*." She pointed in the direction of a half-sunken lobster boat that was a good eighty yards away.

Before I could answer, all four were swimming in the direction of the boat. I didn't think I could dog paddle that far, so I stayed where I was. Then I realized that I couldn't get back on the wharf with that spider in the way. I saw another ladder about thirty feet away, and I paddled over. I'd had enough – after I climbed back up top, I sat with my feet dangling over the edge looking at the gang having fun over at the *Miss Louisa*. Even Timmy had no trouble getting across. I was sure they all thought I was the biggest baby in the world. Happy snuggled up against me.

Mister McGillivery walked by carrying two of the full-up bait buckets. "What's the matter, Eliot, can't swim? What can you do?" I wondered if I should answer that I knew how to blow my nose properly.

He set down the buckets, cupped his hands around his mouth and yelled, "Mary Beth, you git home and do your friggin' chores, girl. I'm going ta town and yer arse better be back before I yam."

A few minutes later, Earl came by and said, "I'll take your gear back, boy. Do you want me to leave your boots and socks?" I looked around at the piles of clothes left by the other kids – there were no boots or socks.

"Take them," I said.

"Be home for dinner by six thirty – remember, we're having something special." He picked up my stuff and left.

Great, I thought, pickled brains? Tears welled up in my eyes. This was all so much worse than I had expected. I had the gift of good imagination. My teacher Mr. Able even wrote "Eliot Dionisi has a rich, if somewhat dark, imagination" on my report card. My parents weren't convinced that the comment was a good thing, but me and Mike and Teddy thought it was the best thing ever. What exactly, I wondered, would be the point of having a gift like that, if real life turned out to be even darker?

I quickly   wiped away

I sniffled,

sucked in some air and
pressed my lips together.

a tear before it had the chance to roll down my cheek.

I was angry with myself – and with everybody else.

After the kids had finished swimming, they joined me on the
wharf. Mary Beth came so close to me, I could have counted the
freckles across the bridge of her nose. "You all right?" she asked.
I wondered if she could tell I'd been sniffling.

"Sure," I said.

"You should've come with us to the *Miss Louisa!*"

"Got a cramp in my leg," I lied.

Mary Beth put both her hands on my shoulders, and tilted her head
to the side. "Next time then," she said. We looked into each other's
eyes. It probably only lasted a second or two, but it seemed like hours.
I couldn't take it anymore and looked down.

That's when I noticed a bruise that went all the way around
the top of Mary Beth's arm. "Did you just get that over at the *Miss
Louisa?*" I asked.

"I don't remember," she said. "What's it to ya?" Her eyes
narrowed and her hands dropped from my shoulders. She seemed an-
noyed. I didn't know what I'd said to cause that reaction.

We both got dressed in silence.

"How far is Earl's place?" I asked.

"Oh, about three or more miles, I guess," said Jack. "We'll stop at Timmy's store along the way."

"Don't you have to be back for chores?" I asked Mary Beth.

"Pa won't be back before eight," she said. "Besides, Ma will cover for me."

When we left the wharf and got onto the road, Happy pushed me over onto the side. I guess he was protecting me from traffic, but the stones were hurting my feet, so I had to look for flat spots with each step. All four Point Aconi kids were walking as though they had leather soles on the bottoms of their feet. Mary Beth looked back and said, "That's OK, Eliot – you'll get used to it." That's what she said about everything! We stopped a couple of times to catch grasshoppers or to carefully select a long blade of grass to hang from our mouths.

Jack and Mary Beth pointed out houses along the way and told me who lived in each one. Eddie and Timmy would add in details like, "They got a new truck last year" or "Mister Paterson works in the mines." Jack started to wave when he saw a green pickup truck coming down the road.

"That's Old Miss Gifford," said Jack. "She'll give us a lift." The truck stopped and Jack shouted, "Can you drop us at What's the Point?" Before Old Miss Gifford had a chance to answer, all four kids had jumped into the cargo bed. Happy leapt in over the tailgate. "C'mon, Eliot," said Jack.

I climbed on the running board and was just lifting my leg over the edge when the truck jerked forward. Mary Beth grabbed my arms and pulled me in. I sat with Eddie, Timmy, and Happy up near the cab. Mary Beth and Jack each took a spot up on the wall of the bed near the tailgate. It was a whole lot better than walking on stones.

After a few short minutes, the truck pulled off the road and came to a stop. We all jumped out and waved our thanks to Old Miss Gifford before she pulled away.

There was a tall, pasty-looking teenager in a black sleeveless T-shirt leaning up against the doorframe of the store. He looked to be sixteen or seventeen. He narrowed his eyes and flicked away a cigarette when he caught sight of us.

"Uh-oh," said Mary Beth. "I was afraid of this – that's Donnie, Jack and Eddie's brother."

"I'll handle this," said Jack. "He's just mad because Pa didn't want him working on the boat this summer. Hey, Donnie," he shouted, "this here kid is Eliot!"

"So that's the wop," he said with a sneer.

"He's a good guy when you get to know him."

"Why the frig would I want to know that little pisser?" asked Donnie.

Happy growled and showed his teeth. I was starting to get that sick feeling in the pit of my stomach again. Great, after crying I was now going to vomit?

"Don't worry," whispered Mary Beth, "just walk right past him and into the store. I'll protect you." I was hoping that the other guys didn't hear that. Even back in Lakefield, it would be kinda strange getting a girl to protect you from a bully.

"But what does he have against me?" I whispered.

"He hates anybody that's new or different," she said. "Not like me, I like different people."

Timmy walked in first and said, "My pah-pa duh-don't like you hangin' round our store."

Donnie curled his lip and mocked Timmy: "Tell your pah-pa to fuh-frig off. And tell him if he's got somethin' to say, ta do it himself, instead of sending his stuh-stuttering dunce."

We started walking towards the entrance of the store under Donnie's vicious stare. I was second to last and Mary Beth was last. When it came my turn, Donnie blocked my way. But he moved away fast when Happy snapped at his pants leg. I quickly made my way through. Mary Beth came next and said something to Donnie in a low angry voice that I couldn't make out.

Donnie growled back louder, "We'll see about dat!" Mary Beth smiled sarcastically and walked past him with Happy at her side.

"What did you say to him?" I whispered.

She snickered and said, "I just told him that I was gonna give him an even worse walloping than the last time if he didn't frig off. I'm not afraid of him," Mary Beth continued. "One time he shoved me hard into a ditch. I hit me head on a rock and it was bleeding bad. I was so

MAD

that I got right up and

PUNCHED

him in the eye.

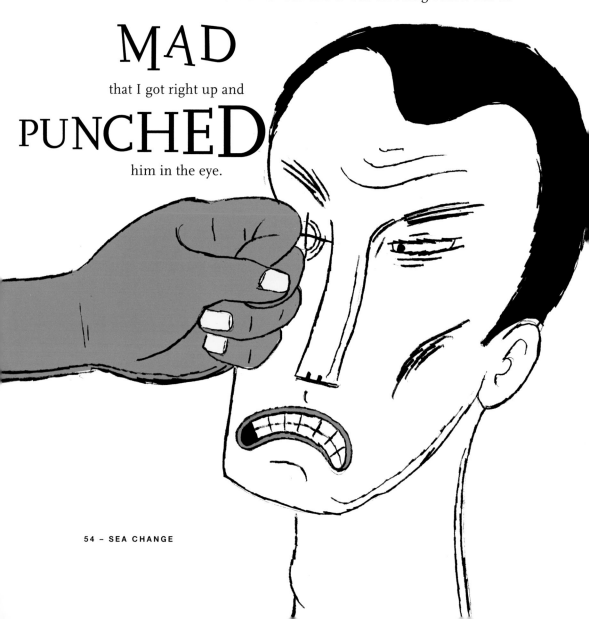

He's never bothered me since." She was smiling, but I was worried that this exchange would make Donnie all the angrier.

What's the Point was a dark little place with three bare light bulbs hanging from a tin ceiling that had been painted over one too many times. There was a long counter along one side. Opposite the counter was a row of wooden shelves that – except for a few large bags of flour and oatmeal – were mostly empty. The shallow shelves that lined the wall behind the counter were stocked with every kind of tobacco and candy imaginable. Standing behind the counter was a pretty girl with long yellow hair and a blue dress – I guessed that she was about my age. I couldn't imagine how a kid my age could be running a store. She came over to us and looked straight at me. "Hi there," she said. "You're Eliot, right? I heard all about you from Timmy. So you're his cool new friend from away, eh? I'm his sister, Penny."

I felt I hardly knew Timmy, but it was nice to know that Timmy thought I was cool. I turned to smile at him, but he was looking down at his shoes, kicking the floor.

"Hi," I said. I decided that I was going to treat the gang with the twenty dollar bill my mom had stuffed into my pocket before I left. "Can I get five of those little bags of chips...and, um, what kind of gum do you have?"

"Oh-oh-oh, get the Buh-Black Cats," said Timmy. "Get them, they're the buh-best."

"And five Black Cats," I said. She added up the order with a stubby yellow pencil on a lined pad of paper.

"That'll be one dollar and thirty-nine cents." I reached into my pocket and slid the soggy twenty dollar bill across the counter. It took her a few seconds to unfold the bill and after she did, she waved it in the air a few times without even asking why it was wet – as if this was a common occurrence. "Eighteen dollars and sixty-one cents is your change," she said with a smile.

"Thanks." I smiled back and shoved the thick wad of bills she handed me into one of my front pockets and the coins into the other.

Then she brought the five bags of chips and five Black Cats to a table at the back corner of the store. I passed out the loot.

"Thanks," each said in turn.

"My pleasure," I said, echoing something I had heard my mom say at times likes this.

I could see that Donnie was no longer standing in the door, but I figured he was waiting just outside. I was worried, but with Happy, Mary Beth, and the rest of the kids on my side, I felt pretty safe.

We all ripped open our bags. "Mmm, these are really good," I said. They were thin, crisp, and really fresh.

When Mary Beth had finished her bag, she went over to the counter and ordered a bottle of cherry soda. Penny reached down into a small chest refrigerator that was located behind the counter. In one skillful motion, she spun the bottle around so it was right-side up, popped off the top, and plunked the soda down on the counter.

Mary Beth slapped some change down on the counter and turned in our direction. "We share! And don't take too much when it's your turn. OK, Jack?"

"Why me?" said Jack.

The pop went around the table twice. Poor Timmy was last and only got a few D R O P S on his second turn.

Then we unwrapped our gum and tossed it into our mouths. It tasted different from any gum I had ever had. Sort of a combination of soap and licorice, but I liked it.

"Who is Old Miss Gifford?" I asked.

"Oh, she's the teacher," said Mary Beth. "She's been teaching here since my pa was little. She knows everything about everything. Ma says she helps Point Aconi people when they're in trouble, but Pa says she just loves sticking her nose in everybody's business. She's never even been married."

"And she's against Bushwhacker Coal moving in here and buying up the properties," said Jack.

"She guh-goes on and on and on a-buh-bout that," said Timmy.

"My grandmother mentioned Bushwhacker Coal," I said. "What do they do?"

"They're a company that strip-mines coal," said Jack. "They're the reason the pond got poisoned. Their trucks load up on the back road and rumble through here every day. That's why the road's so beat up and everything's so dusty all the time. They tried to buy our property."

"Us too," said Timmy. "But Ma says they didn't offer us enough money for it."

After that, we hung around the table chewing our gum in silence. We lingered a long time before saying goodbye to Penny and walking out into the glaring sunlight.

The scene was much worse than I could have imagined: Donnie had two tough-looking friends with him. One toothless boy grinned and waved mockingly at us from a white pickup truck. Donnie sat on the cab and casually smoked a cigarette. The smoke twisted in the air like an agitated snake ready to strike. My heart sank when I heard him hiss at me through the smoke.

"Oh, cripes," said Mary Beth, "that's Billy Reid and Dave Gillespie."

"Frig! What're we gonna do now?" said Jack.

"Well, well, well, look at that," said one of them – a big kid in a black T-shirt who I later learned was Billy Reid. "The little maggots found a new maggot." They all laughed.

"Get lost and take your dumb friends with you or I'm telling Pa," said Jack to his brother Donnie. "Me too," said Eddie.

"Pa's not gonna give a rat's arse about your wop friend," said Donnie. "And anyways, I'm gonna beat the little stuck-up frigger to within an inch of his life." One of the boys grabbed a baseball bat from the back of the truck. They began to walk in our direction. I wondered if I should stand in front of Mary Beth to protect her, but I couldn't move my feet. Happy slunk towards the boys and snarled at them.

Then Timmy stepped out in front. He marched straight up to Donnie and looked him in the eyes. "Guh-get off our puh-property," he said, "or I'll call my puh-pa." I couldn't believe it. Timmy, the smallest kid of the lot, was also the bravest.

"Look at that," said Donnie, "the skinny halfwit thinks he's gonna protect the little wop. I'm always happy to give our little Timmy another thumpin' on the noggin."

They shared another little laugh. But before they could come any closer, Old Miss Gifford's green pickup pulled in and stopped right between the two groups. Even through the window of her truck, I could see she was pretty fat, with a wild mop of curly black-and-silver hair, but from the moment she rolled herself out of the cab, I knew she was a dream come true.

"Everything OK here?" she asked.

"Miss Gifford, can you give us a ride down to Earl's place?" asked Mary Beth.

Old Miss Gifford studied Donnie and his friends. After a long pause, she said, "Hop in, kids."

Penny was standing in the door of What's the Point. Miss Gifford looked over at her and said, "You'd better close up now, Penny." Without a word, Penny shuttered the door and locked it from within.

We all jumped into the back of Miss Gifford's truck. We had to call Happy a few times because he was still snarling at the boy with the bat, but he finally came.

Miss Gifford looked over at Donnie and his friends, and said:

"you boys better go home before you get yourself in serious trouble. as it is, i'm going to have a talk with your parents. do you hear me?"

Then she rolled herself back into the cab of her truck and shifted the idling engine into reverse.

"That was a close one," said Timmy.

I was still shaking as the truck pulled away, but with What's the Point getting smaller behind us, I felt a little better.

Then, on a wisp of wind, I heard Donnie call, "You're dead, wop. You might not know it yet, but you're already dead."

I slumped into a corner. After a few short minutes, Miss Gifford pulled the truck into Earl's driveway and stopped near the entrance. We jumped out and Jack said thanks.

"You kids stay away from those boys, do you hear?" said Miss Gifford. "And if they give you any more trouble, you tell me and I'll take care of it. OK then?"

"We will, Miss Gifford!" said Mary Beth as the truck pulled away.

We walked up Earl's long driveway and found a sunny place near the barn to sit and talk. I had never been so frightened in my life. Donnie and his friends were actually going to hurt me. With a baseball bat. The kids tried to cheer me up with talk about all the adventures we'd have that summer. We'd have a clambake on the mud flats, we'd walk to the back beach, we'd pick blueberries, and we'd go exploring around the lighthouse. But I was thinking that Donnie would probably get to me before we got the chance to do any of these things.

Out at the road, the white pickup passed back and forth at the end of Earl's driveway. I looked away, but I could still hear the growl of its engine and the hiss of tires.

After a long silence, Mary Beth stood up and said, "I'd better get going. Ma will need help with the little ones."

"Take the back path home," said Jack.

"I will," she said and started out. Eddie and Jack said they'd better get back too. After that, only Timmy and I were left – the two losers on Donnie's shortlist.

"Thanks for standing up for me," I said. "That was very brave."

"Oh, you woulda duh-done it for me," he said. But I knew it wasn't true.

We sat there in silence with long faces. When we finally stood up, we caught sight of the white pickup again – rolling by, ever so slowly. "Do you want to come in?" I asked Timmy.

"Really?" he asked with wide eyes and an enormous grin. It was like nobody had ever asked him to do anything before.

The screen door shut behind us with a thwack. Earl's voice rolled down from somewhere up high: "Up here, kid." I looked around and saw a yellow light coming from a narrow staircase in the very back of the porch. Compared to what was waiting for me outside, facing up to Uncle Earl didn't seem like such a big deal.

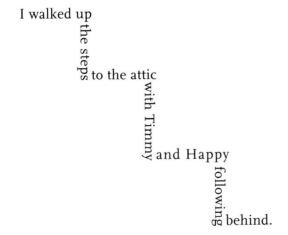

I walked up the steps to the attic with Timmy and Happy following behind.

And when I surfaced, I couldn't believe my eyes.

10

Uncle Earl was wearing a pair of wire-framed reading glasses and sitting in a well-used leather chair. He was reading a tattered book by the light of a dim lamp. He looked so different there, away from his boat. More like the kind of uncle you'd tell a secret to than the kind who'd make you shovel rotten mackerel. There were books all around him, and as my eyes adjusted to the light, I could see that every wall had a bookcase and they were all stuffed with books. Books and more books sat in stacks on the floor and surrounded an old metal trunk that Uncle Earl was using as a footstool.

I stood there in silence for a long time, just looking. Timmy was nudging me from behind, but I didn't make a move. Finally Earl looked up. "This was your Great-grandmother Minnie's library. She loved to come up here and read for hours on end. And this book," he said, handing me the one he was holding, "is your Great-great-grandfather Steen's diary."

"Why are you showing it to me?"

"Because I noticed you're a reader, Eliot. Aren't you?"

The last bits of daylight that came in through
a tiny attic window
made the gold lettering on all the book spines shimmer.

Honestly, I was surprised he noticed anything about me other than my height and how useless I was. "I am," I said cautiously. I realized that this was the first time he'd ever called me by my name.

"Me too," he said. "You have a look through the diary and bring down any other books you might want to read. I'm going to finish cooking our special dinner. I'll call you when it's ready. I see you brought home a friend. Can you join us for dinner, Timmy?"

On June 27ᵗʰ, we arose at seve and set out in Mister Clopp blue dory to see some vacan property at a place called ᵗ ᵘnt. Cousin Eddie fee ᵘght fill our needs We skirted the coastline and rowed for two hours before taking notice of a dark line of clouds movin in over the sea from the w We landed the dory on beach that was covered long strands of yellow

"I duh-dunno if I should," said Timmy.

"Of course you should. I'll call your ma and tell her you're having dinner here," said Earl. "C'mon, Happy!" But Happy didn't move a muscle. "Well now," said Earl, "it looks like you have two new friends." He looked a little bewildered as he disappeared down the steps.

I sat down in the chair and began to leaf through the diary. It was leather-bound and the pages were handwritten.

and green seaweed. We took refuge under a row of Alders. Although the Alders provided little cover, the storm passed quickly and we wer[e] to resume our journ[ey]

We encountered some rough waves as we made our way around Alder Point, but as we crossed the mouth of Little Bras d'Or, the waves calmed down Considerably We dropped our lines

"What duh-does it sah-say?" Timmy asked.

"I'm not sure," I said. The date on the cover was 1862. On a few of the pages was a story about how the Purvis clan came upon "The Point," with its sheltered river, fertile fishing grounds, and beautiful beaches. The rest of it wasn't exactly a diary – more like a collection of recipes, cures, and step-by-step instructions. There were directions for making unusual things like invisible ink and maple syrup, but the page that caught my eye was titled "A Poultice for Drawing Out the Cancer." Could it be that a real cure for cancer was hidden in the pages of this book? There were also cures for whooping cough, poison ivy, scarlet fever, and a hundred other things.

"Look at this, Timmy," I said, pointing to a place further along in the book. "We can make GINGER BEER!" "My mah-ma said I'm not allowed to drink buh-beer." I laughed and told him it wasn't that kind of beer.

I set the diary down on the trunk, walked over to the shelves, and pulled out a dusty clothbound copy of *Treasure Island*, one of my favorite books of all time. "Has your mother ever read this book to you?" I asked.

Timmy shook his head. "What's it about?"

I motioned for him to sit with me on the leather chair, which was big enough for both of us if we squeezed together. Then I cleared my throat and began to read the story of young Jim Hawkins. "SQUIRE TRELAWNEY, Dr. Livesey, and the rest of these gentlemen having asked me to write down the whole particulars about Treasure Island, from the beginning to the end, keeping nothing back but the bearings of the island, and that only because there is still treasure not yet lifted..."As I read aloud, I tried to make my voice change from high and sweet to low and dark, the way my mom always did when she read to me. Each time I got to a "Yo-ho-ho and a bottle of rum!" I yelled it loud enough to make Timmy jump off his seat.

After I read the part in chapter two where Black Dog holds his hand up to show his missing fingers, I glanced over, and Timmy's eyes were as round as saucers. Later, when we came to the sword fight between Black Dog and Billy Bones, he softly squeaked, "Oh, no!" Some of the words were pretty difficult, even for me, but Timmy wasn't missing a beat.

Just as I began chapter four, Earl called up the stairs that dinner was ready. By then I was really hungry.

"Wah-when can we read muh-more?" said Timmy.

"Maybe after dinner," I said.

Downstairs, the kitchen looked much worse than I could have imagined – the table was completely covered with newspaper, and at each place lay a bright orange lobster with steam rising from it. There was a nutcracker and a fork sitting beside each lobster – and a little dish with melted butter. "It's a good thing I brought three lobsters home," said Earl. "I was going to use the third to make lobster rolls for our lunch tomorrow. No matter, we have peanut butter and jam. Have a seat. I also made a bowl of Swiss chard – fresh from the garden!" It smelled good in the kitchen, warm and homey, but I couldn't stop staring into the bulbous black eyes of the creature that was supposed to be my dinner. Two long antennae stuck out of its face. It looked like it might crawl across the table and eat me.

Timmy sat right down and said, "Yum!" He pulled off the tail and cracked it open. Earl did the same.

"Sit! Eat!" said Earl.

I sat down and fumbled with my napkin. I took my time making it into a bib, hoping Timmy and Earl wouldn't notice.

"Yo-ho-ho!" Timmy suddenly shouted. "You've nah-never had lobster before, hu-huh?"

"Sure I have," I lied. "Hundreds of times."

Timmy cocked his head to the side. Instead of arguing with me, he just said, "Then you muh-must already know how to duh-do this," and ripped the tail off my lobster. I was relieved to have Timmy come to my rescue, so I wouldn't look like a fool in front of my uncle for the thousandth time. I watched him expertly squeeze the tail so it cracked lengthwise and then pry the shell open from the bottom. Juice was spraying everywhere – even into my eye. With his fork, he pulled the white meat from the tail and left it on my plate.

"Try it," he said. "It's gah-good! Puh-pick it up with your fingers!" I picked up the spongy thing and smelled it.

"Dip it in the butter," said Earl. He was looking at me like he was about to say something mean, so I thought I'd better try it. Besides, my father always said that anything tastes good with butter on it – even shoe leather.

I picked it up, dipped it in the butter, and took a tiny bite. It didn't taste too fishy. It was sort of sweet. I dipped it again and took another little bite. It was actually pretty good – soft and warm and comforting, as good as anything I could remember eating back home. In no time I finished the whole tail.

"So, how was your afternoon?" asked Earl. I looked over at Timmy, wondering if I should try to tell Earl what happened at the store.

Timmy was still lost in the meal. He had a big, satisfied smile on his face, with the last bits of butter shining at the corners of his mouth. For a skinny kid, he could sure pack away a lot. "That was so guh-good," he said. "Thank you very muh-much, sir."

"My pleasure," said Earl. The way Earl said that reminded me of my mother. I wondered if she picked it up from Earl when she stayed here as a little kid. Maybe, I thought, they both got it from my great-grand-mother, Minnie. And maybe she got it from my great-great-grandfather, Steen – the guy who made the diary.

"That diary book you showed me was cool," I said. "I really liked the part about the Purvis clan finding Point Aconi. Are there many Purvises left around here?"

"I'm the last," said Earl.

"Really?"

"Yes, boy, and I'm going to take it out in style."

"Is it OK if we go back up to the attic now?"

"Not today," said Earl. "I think you'd better head home, Timmy. Eliot has another early day tomorrow."

After dinner, I walked Timmy out and onto the driveway. There were even more stars in the sky than the night before. Millions and millions of them! I had never seen the Milky Way look so big or bright. Timmy saw me looking up and said, "They're there juh-just for us."

"What do you mean?" I said.

"If we weren't here, nuh-nobody would see 'em," he said simply.

"So, if we weren't here looking at them, they might not be there?" I said with a laugh.

"Mah-maybe," he said. "Can we read muh-more of *Treasure Island* tomorrow?"

"I hope so," I said.

"And duh-don't worry about duh-Donnie and his friends," he said. "They only mah-meant to scare us." I was beginning to think that there was a lot of stuff going on inside Timmy's head, more than the others gave him credit for.

I tried to think of nice things while I lay in bed that night: the stars in the sky, the library in the attic, the taste of lobster dipped in butter, but I was too tired to even remember why I had been crying, or who was my friend and who was not.

In the middle of the night, drenched in sweat, I woke up from a dream in which Donnie McLeod, dressed like a pirate, was chasing me all around What's the Point with a cutlass, poking me in the back. Everyone in Point Aconi, including Uncle Earl, Old Miss Gifford, Timmy, and Mary Beth, was standing there, watching and laughing every time I jumped up in pain. They all seemed to think it was very funny.

11

The next day started out pretty much like the last one. I had the job of filling up the bait buckets with rotting fish. It was, I knew, the only job they thought I could actually do. It was just as horrible as the first time, but at least I didn't throw up.

After I hauled the buckets down to the *YNOT*, I decided to try working the ropes. I practiced at it while Earl and Mister McGillivery were fiddling with the *YNOT*'s engine. It was really pretty easy, once you got the hang of it. All you had to do was push the end of the rope out through the first loop, and then pull hard. When you pulled, the rest of the loops just came undone. I jumped up when I heard the *YNOT*'s engine come to life with that deep, watery growl.

"Cast off, Dermot," said Earl.

"Let me do it," I said. I already had the first one untied, so I tossed it down to Mister McGillivery and quickly untied the other one and tossed it, too. Mister McGillivery looked back up at me with a dumb, slack-jawed expression.

"Good work, Eliot," said Earl. Then I scampered down the

ladder like an expert, and took my place with Happy in the bow. It was all I could do to stop myself from sticking out my tongue at Mister McGillivery.

This time, I couldn't see the bottom because the surface of the water was a bit choppy. By the time we saw the first buoy, the waves were getting pretty high. I had to hold onto the gunwale to keep from falling over.

I stepped forward and told Earl that I was ready to get back to the job of putting on the rubber bands. And that day, I only dropped two lobsters, but I picked them right back up again. When we'd finished the first two lines of traps, Earl looked over at me and said, "What got into you, kid?"

"I dunno," I said with a grin, "maybe I just needed to eat one first." I looked over at Mister McGillivery. He leered back and muttered something indecipherable.

At lunch, Earl and I ate our peanut butter and jam sandwiches on the little bench near the bow. Mister McGillivery sat in the stern with his back turned away.

I was amazed at the amount of food he kept pulling from his metal lunch box.

I turned away and asked Earl if he knew anything about Old Miss Gifford.

"You mean Mabel," said Earl. "Her name is Mabel."

"I guess," I said. "She gave us a lift down to What's the Point yesterday."

"Oh, I see," said Earl. "Well, let me tell you a little bit about Mabel. In my mind, she's better 'n' probably stronger than just about anybody in Point Aconi. She's the salt of the earth. We don't have enough of her type around here."

"The kids also told me a little about Bushwhacker Coal," I said.

"Oh, those snakes," said Earl. "They're a different kettle of fish. They don't give a tinker's cuss about the people in Point Aconi. They just want to suck up all our land and strip it clean. They'll do just about anything to get down to the coal the cheapest way they can."

Earl was starting to turn red. "But Mabel," he went on, "tries to remind our people that they can't buy a better way of life than what we have here – especially for the pittance Bushwhacker is offering for our homes. They hate her for that."

By this time he was spitting out angry bits of bread and jam. "And the government," he added, "they're against her too. They say Bush-whacker will create jobs in Point Aconi. But Mabel says that there'll be no real jobs, just a couple of guys from away working bulldozers. And I agree with her, Eliot. God knows they've already made a mess of things out by the old back road. It used to be beautiful back there. Now it looks like the surface of the moon."

I knew then that I couldn't help Grandmother McNeil with her plan to get Earl to sell the house. What would be the point of telling Earl that Point Aconi was crap? He loved Point Aconi – and the people who made it their home.

I wasn't sure what it all meant, but it was clear to me that Bush-whacker Coal and some of the people in Point Aconi were against Old Miss Gifford. Even the government was against her. But I liked her. And Earl seemed to like her a lot.

After I finished my sandwich, I stood up and had to sit right back down again. The sway from the waves was starting to make me feel sick. I staggered over to the gunwale and rested there for a minute. Then I started to puke over the side. First, I puked up the peanut butter and jam sandwich. After that came breakfast. Then I was just heaving over and over, but only a little bit of yellowish-green bile was coming up. That was the worst part. All the while, I could hear Mister McGillivery laughing.

Why did this have to happen? Just when I thought things were getting a little better. After the gagging stopped, I felt weak and collapsed back onto the little bench.

Earl came over and sat down beside me. He patted me on the shoul-der and said, "After this, you'll have earned your sea legs. And you'll likely never be sick again. Congratulations!"

"Really?" I asked.

"Think of it as a rite of passage. It happened
to me when I was about your age." I reached
over and gave him a hug, but he pulled away.
"The back, boy! Remember, I've got a bad back.
Listen," he said, "you did a good job today and
I'm proud of you. You stay here and rest for a
while – Dermot and me will finish the third line."

When we arrived back at the wharf, the gang
was waiting for me. Timmy was all excited and
wanted to be the first to give the news.

"Duh-Donnie went on his dah-dad's boat this
morning. Old Miss Guh-Gifford talked to them
yesterday, and now his dah-dad took him buh-back
on the water. Just to keep a wuh-watch on him
I think. Anyway, he won't buh-be around so much
now. See, I tah-told you everything would
buh-be OK," said Timmy. He seemed so happy,
I stopped myself from saying anything about
what might happen whenever he was around.

Once again, Jack was the first one in the water, followed by Mary
Beth, Eddie, and Timmy. As I stood on the wharf looking down at
the twelve-foot drop, they yelled, "Jump, Eliot, jump! You can do it!"
So I jumped. It wasn't the most graceful dive, and I sort of landed
on my stomach, and it stung, but I did it.

"Yay!" they yelled. We swam around the wharf
for a bit. I told them I was too tired to swim over
to the *Miss Louisa* but that they should go ahead.
I was just happy to have jumped into the water.

After they swam away, I noticed that the fat
spider was still camping out on the ladder.
I made my way over to the other ladder and
climbed back up onto the wharf. I just sat there
smiling and soaking up the sun. Although the
threat of Donnie still hung heavy, it had been a good day.

I had four new friends
and Earl was proud of me.

When the gang swam back and
joined me on the wharf, I noticed a fresh bruise on Mary Beth.

"How did you get hurt this time?" I asked, pointing to her finger. "What's it to ya?"

"Lay off it!" she said, swatting at my finger.

She seemed so angry I was taken aback.

"I'm just worried about you, that's all," I said.

"Well don't be worrying," she said.

"Isn't anything for you to worry about, Eliot Dionisi."

I watched her walk away and then I found a rock on the ground

that I gave a great big kick. Sometimes she seemed to like me

and sometimes she seemed to hate me.

I was very confused.

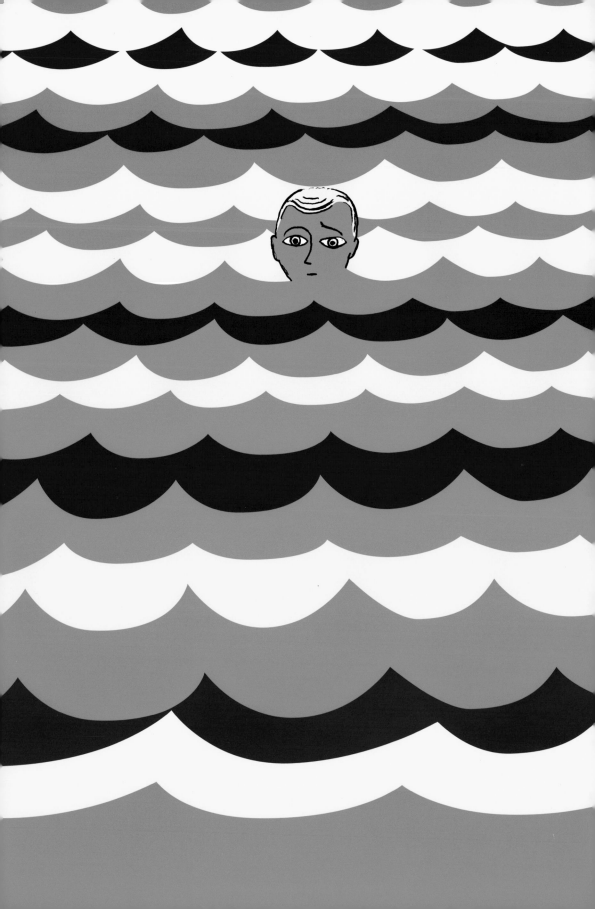

PART 2

12

After only a few weeks, I could haul up the lobster traps and bait
them all by myself. Even better, my hands and feet were covered
in calluses. I could walk or run wherever I wanted – in bare feet.
And each day I got a little better at diving off the wharf. I could even
do a cannonball. But I was still too scared to make the swim over to
the *Miss Louisa*. I even found time to write two postcards. I told my
parents how horrible everything was and asked them if they could
send another twenty dollars. I told Mike and Teddy how wonderful
everything was and that I even had a girlfriend. Both postcards
were only partly true. Maybe I didn't really need another twenty dollars
and maybe Mary Beth wasn't really my girlfriend. Yet. Still, it was true
that some things were pretty wonderful and some things were pretty
awful. I just hoped Mike and Teddy wouldn't share the postcard I sent
them with my parents – or the other way around.

One night, Earl told me that lobster season was over and that we
were going to switch over to jigging cod. On the last day of lobster
season, we pulled all the traps into the boat and piled them in

a
giant
pyramid
on the stern.
Mister McGillivery
lashed them with rope so
they wouldn't fall overboard.
After we got them all back to the
wharf, we stacked them in Earl's truck
and then stacked them again in his backyard.
McGillivery worked up quite a sweat – I was
impressed by how physically strong he was and better
understood why he had been my uncle's partner for so long.

That Monday, we went jigging cod for the first time. Because we used metal lures, we didn't need the rotting fish from the bait shack anymore. It should have been a big relief, but by then I almost missed the maggot run. I was so good at it.

When we started out that first morning, it was – for the most part – like any other day. Gradually, the sea became very rough. When the YNOT

was on the crest of a wave we could look out in all directions, but when it slid down into a trough, we were surrounded by the sea – twenty and thirty feet above our heads.

We reached a spot that Earl thought would be good for cod, and he shut down the engine. Mister McGillivery and Earl dropped their lines over the side.

Earl called over to me: "Eliot, when you're ready, this is how you do it. You drop your line and let it sink all the way down to the bottom. Then you pull it up about a half a fathom. Then you jig, like this." He looped the line around his gloved hand and pulled up and down, about two feet each time.

"Got one!" exclaimed Mister McGillivery. He pulled the codfish all the way to the surface, and put a net under it. "That's queer," he said. "The tail end is bit right off." Earl pulled the next one to the surface and it was the same thing – a good-sized cod with the tail end bitten off. "Must be dogfish getting 'em on the way up," said Mister McGillivery.

"We'd better find another spot," said Earl. He cranked the engine and took the *YNOT* out farther, to another one of his favorite spots.

This time, all three of us dropped lines. I caught one almost immediately and pulled it to the surface. It was the same thing – only half a cod. "I never seen the likes of it," said Mister McGillivery. Again and again the same thing happened.

"Pull in your lines," said Earl. "We'll go to another spot." I looked down into the water and I saw a giant white fish following Mister McGillivery's line up to the surface. Earl looked down and said, "Jumping Jesus, it's a great white. Stay away from the edge, Eliot." I stepped back. The shark surfaced for a second and then went back down. "He must've followed us from the last spot," said Earl.

"Look down there, boy, chance of a lifetime," said Mister McGillivery.

We all looked over the edge and could see the shark.

He was about five feet below the surface and was swimming

slowly under the *YNOT*.

Happy looked down over the transom and started to bark.

"He must be a good twenty-five-footer," said Earl.

"Well, boys, I'm afraid there'll be no catch today."

He started the engine and we headed back in.

"Won't he follow us again?" I asked.

"Nah, he'll give up. The bay is too shallow for the likes of him," said Earl. As we headed in, the rollers were still carrying the *YNOT* way up and back down again, but the motion wasn't making me sick. I joined Earl in the wheelhouse and told him so.

"Good then, you've got your sea legs," said Earl. I stayed with Earl and Happy in the wheelhouse all the way back in. Mister McGillivery sat on the stern deck chewing a big wad of tobacco and spitting bits of it out now and then.

Because we arrived back at the dock earlier than normal, Mary Beth and the kids hadn't yet turned up for our daily swim. Earl and Mister McGillivery were telling a few fishermen who were working on the docks about the great white shark.

"I saw one as long as twenty feet," said one.

"You wanna stay away from them fellas," said another.

After the powwow, Earl came over and asked me if I wanted a ride back.

"Nah," I said, "I'll wait for Timmy, Mary Beth, and the kids. Today's the day I'm going to swim over to the *Miss Louisa*."

"Well, you be careful," said Earl. "Stay with Eliot," Earl said to Happy. But there was no need, for by now, Happy and I were inseparable.

I was sitting with my legs dangling over the edge of the wharf, preparing for my big swim, when somebody tapped me on the shoulder. It was Donnie. "Hello, wop," he said. He was swinging a gaff back and forth in his left hand. Then he grabbed the center of the handle with his right hand and held it over my head. "Where are all your friends now?"

Before I could think of what to say or do, I had jumped into the water, clothes and all. I started swimming as fast as I could towards the *Miss Louisa*.

After I got out about fifteen feet, I heard a loud swoosh close by. Donnie had thrown the gaff at me like a spear. "I'll get you, you little frig," he called. Just then, I felt something brush up against my stomach. All at once, the image of the great white shark following the line up to the surface came into my head. Didn't the shark follow the *YNOT* from one place to the next? Couldn't he have followed it back to the wharf? I panicked and slid under the water.

When I came back up, I splashed around in terror for a moment before finding the strength to swim a few more strokes, but I couldn't shake the image of the ghostly white shark.

Earl said that the bay was too shallow for a big shark, but hadn't I seen TV programs that showed a shark attacking people on a shallow beach? I gulped some water and swam a few more strokes.

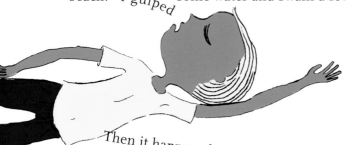

Then it happened again – something brushed by my stomach. This time I really panicked and started screaming. I tried to call for help, but only a little squeak came out of my mouth. There was no way I was going to be able to make it all the way to the *Miss Louisa*.

At that moment, Happy appeared from nowhere. Having him there in the water calmed me down a little. I began swimming beside him. I didn't know where we were going – I just followed. I looked up at the wharf, but Donnie was gone.

After a long time, we reached the shore. I pulled myself up onto the rocks and collapsed. Happy was on his side, panting and breathing heavily, so I rolled over and patted him gently. I looked into his brown eyes and whispered, "You saved my life, you old, mangy dog. Thank you." He licked my nose. I gave him a long hug. I probably squeezed too hard, but he just wagged his tail and licked me again.

We climbed up the rocks and found our way back onto the wharf. Donnie was nowhere in sight. I looked over at the spot where it had all happened. I half expected to see the shark, but there was just a bed of seaweed with the tops poking up through the surface of the water.

That's what brushed my stomach, I thought – seaweed! I felt embarrassed. I looked over again and saw the gaff that Donnie threw. It was tangled in the weeds. What if Donnie saw everything? He probably thought I screamed like a baby because I was afraid of the weeds. He'd have a wonderful time telling the whole story to Mary Beth and the gang. I sat down on the wharf and groaned. I must've looked like a drowned rat. Happy nudged my cheek with his cold, wet nose. I patted his head as a hand reached out and touched my shoulder. It was Mary Beth. She sat down beside me and gave me one of her long looks. "Are you all right, Eliot?" she asked. "You look like you've seen a ghost."

She looked into my eyes as she touched my cheek with the back of her hand.

Then she kissed me on the lips.

13

I started out wishing the summer would fly by, but after that kiss,
I wanted it to slow down. I wanted more kisses and more swims
and more days on the *YNOT*. But as each day passed, the quicker
it seemed to go. The weather was perfect – it didn't rain more than
twice that entire August. Each workday, I caught almost as many
codfish as Earl and Mister McGillivery. It made me feel good to know
that I was pulling my own weight. I was happy to have a circle of
four close friends, but I felt closest to Mary Beth and Timmy.

I got to kiss Mary Beth three more times, and I spent many evenings
with Timmy in Great-grandmother Purvis's library. We finished
Treasure Island, The Adventures of Tom Sawyer, and *Never Cry Wolf.*
We did almost everything on our list. We explored the lighthouse,
we picked blueberries, and one evening we had a clambake on
the mud flats. The only thing we hadn't done yet was go to the beach
out by the old back road. Earl finally convinced me to try cow's tongue.
It was just awful.

On a Saturday afternoon, just a few days before I had to go

back to Lakefield, Mary Beth, Timmy, and I decided to have a picnic behind Mary Beth's house. We found a place that was hidden in the long grass. I brought peanut butter and jam sandwiches, Timmy brought a quart of blueberries, and Mary Beth brought a blanket. I also brought an illustrated edition of *The Time Machine* by H.G. Wells.

Mary Beth sat with her arm draped over my shoulder as I read aloud from the book. The Morlocks, we learned, were an evil, ape-like people who lived underground in the distant future. They feasted on the Eloi, a gentle people who lived up on the surface. As usual, Timmy was spellbound.

"Point Aconi hah-has Muh-Morlocks and Eloi," said Timmy.

"I guess so," I said. "In a way."

"Who are the Morlocks living here in Point Aconi?" asked Mary Beth.

"Donnie's one of the Muh-Morlocks for sure," said Timmy.

"The people who own Bushwhacker Coal are all Morlocks," I said. They both nodded.

"Wah-We are the Eloi of Puh-Point Aconi," said Timmy. "Us and Old Mah-Miss Gifford and Earl and Puh-Penny and the rest of my family."

"But the Eloi don't fight back," said Mary Beth.

"Maybe they do," I said, "later in the book."

We were interrupted by the sound of people talking in the distance. I peeked up over the top of the grass and saw Mister McGillivery and another man. Mary Beth looked up.

"That's the man from Bushwhacker Coal talking to Pa," she said. Mister McGillivery and the man came closer and stopped about ten feet away. We ducked down. We could hear everything they were saying.

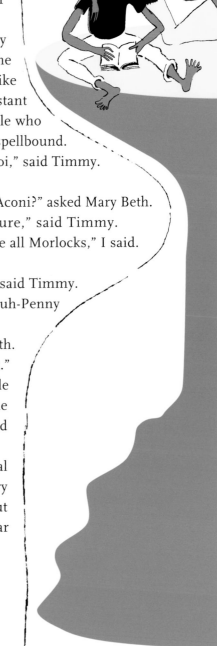

"I own dis here strip of land," said Mister McGillivery, "all the way up from the road and down to the water. And for the right price you can own 'er."

"What's your idea of the right price?" asked the man.

"They're talking about selling your place," I whispered.

"Ma won't let Pa do that," she whispered. "It's her people's land."

"What if he doesn't tell her," I whispered back, "and sells it anyway?" Mary Beth shook her head, but she looked worried. Just then, Timmy sneezed.

"Who the frig is that?" barked Mister McGillivery.

"Who the frig is what?" asked the man.

"You didn't hear it?" asked Mister McGillivery.

"Oh, maybe a bird or a squirrel. Are you all right, Mister McGillivery?" asked the man.

"Course I'm all right," said Mister McGillivery. I wondered if the man from Bushwhacker Coal was the same man who Grandmother McNeil had almost married. I remembered her saying on the way in that I wouldn't be here today if she'd married him. I also remembered thinking that I didn't care in the least if Point Aconi got bought up by Bushwhacker back then, but now the thought made me angry. Where would everybody go? It was like Earl and Old Miss Gifford said, the people here wouldn't be able to buy a new way of life better than what they had – no matter how much Bushwhacker offered them for the land.

After the two men walked away, I said,

"Mary Beth, you'd better tell your ma about this."

"I will," she said. "I will."

The next morning, Mary Beth, Timmy, and I met in secret out on the old back road. Before I left the house, I put on my bathing suit, pulled on my jeans and T-shirt, and rolled my mermaid towel under my arm. It was Sunday, and Earl always slept in on Sundays – if you can call getting up at seven thirty sleeping in. I snuck out as quietly as a mouse. Even Happy didn't wake up.

We walked the five long miles to the back beach. Along the way, we passed the Bushwhacker strip mine. It was closed on Sunday, so we walked up to the entrance and looked in between the padlocked gates. Everything was dead. Not a tree or even a small patch of green could be seen, just two yellow bulldozers sitting in a vast and empty landscape of mud and rock. It really did look like the surface of the moon, just like Earl said.

"That's wah-what they want to dah-do to the rest of Point Aconi," said Timmy.

"We can't let that happen," said Mary Beth.

"Did you tell your ma that your pa met with the man from Bushwhacker Coal?" I asked her.

"No."

"You should, you know."

"I know."

After that, we walked along in silence. When we arrived at the beach, there was nobody else around. I spread out my mermaid towel on the sand and we sat for a while listening to the waves crashing in. Mary Beth peeled down to her bathing suit and ran down to the surf. Timmy and I followed her into the water. Each time we walked out a little way, a giant wave would knock us over. We crawled up to the edge of the surf and made a fort with a moat around it. After an extra-large wave washed away our fort, we walked along the beach collecting bits of things that the waves had washed ashore.

Mary Beth collected seashells, and I looked for pieces of smooth glass. The most common pieces were clear, but a few special ones were bottle green and cobalt blue. Timmy wanted to help us with our collections and ran off to the far end to find more of both.

When Mary Beth and I sat back down on the mermaid towel, I noticed a new bruise on her back. It looked fresh and blue and tender.

"Mary Beth," I said, "I want to know. You have to tell me."

"Know what?" she said. I put my finger on the bruise and traced its outline, like a map.

She stared ahead at the waves crashing on the beach.

"Pa came home drunk last night," she said. Then she lifted her hair and showed me another bruise on the back of her neck. "And that's all you need to know."

She didn't look mad, but I felt mad enough for both of us.

"He's...he's a monster, Mary Beth! I'm going to talk to him, and then I'm going to tell Uncle Earl."

"No you won't," she said. "That's why I didn't want to tell you. It'll only make it worse for me."

"But..." I said.

"But nothing! What do you think would happen if he knew I'd told someone? You're not from around here, Eliot. You don't know anything."

I
wanted
to argue
with her, but I
didn't know what
else to say. On the way
back, Timmy chattered
away, while Mary Beth and I
were lost in thought. I kept thinking about ways to confront Mister
McGillivery myself. I wanted to do
something to make him stop hurting
her, but at the same time, I didn't want
to make things any worse for Mary Beth.
As we came up to Earl's driveway, Timmy turned
for home. "Bye, Timmy," we waved him off.
Mary Beth looked at me and said, "Don't worry, Eliot.
I'm tough. I can take it." For the first time in weeks, I felt
I was about to cry.
"I'm used to it, you know," she said again. "I can take it."
She put a hand on my cheek, and I realized she was trying
to comfort me. A wave of anger and frustration came
over me. The next thing I knew, tears were cascading
down my cheeks and I was sobbing.
"Here, this is for you," I said, wrapping the
mermaid towel around her shoulders. Then
I turned around and ran into Earl's
house, the porch door slamming
behind me.

14

That night a big storm swept in from the ocean. For the first hour or so, the windows would light up with a sudden flash. Each flash was followed by a series of loud thunderclaps that shook the house and rattled the windows. The whole time I was curled up in a little ball, shivering under my covers. Sometimes it was so loud I thought the storm must be just above my bed. In time, it died down, but I could still hear thunder off in the distance, probably rattling the windows of some poor kid in another part of Nova Scotia.

The next day, I couldn't even look at Mister McGillivery. I was filled to the brim with hatred and disgust. As usual, he was happily spitting tobacco, snorting and grunting.

"What's wrong with you?" asked Earl.

"Nothing," I said.

"You haven't said a thing all morning. Are you sad about going back to Lakefield?" he asked.

"Yes and no," I said.

"I picked up a tub of your favorite dessert, Butterscotch Ripple."

If only I could tell Earl about Mary Beth. But how could I? If it
came out, Mister McGillivery would probably beat Mary Beth for
telling. He'd probably take whatever he could get for the land and
run. I'd never see Mary Beth or Timmy again. And if Bushwhacker
Coal got McGillivery's land, Earl would probably blame me. Maybe
the people in Point Aconi would blame Earl for inviting me here.
If only my mom were here, she'd know what to do. I was lost in
my thoughts, and the day passed by quickly. Before I knew it, both
crates were filled with cod, and we were heading back in. The whole
time I was trying to figure out how to help Mary Beth. Then I
remembered Old Miss Gifford. Maybe, I thought, I should talk to her.

When we arrived back at the wharf, I told the kids that I wasn't
feeling well. "I'm going to hitch a ride with Earl back home," I said.

"Do ya want to go swimmin' at the Sandy Spot later on?" asked
Mary Beth.

"Sure," I said.

As we pulled into Earl's driveway, I told him that I wanted to be
alone for a while – and that I was going for a walk.

"OK," he said. "Can I do anything?"

"I don't think so," I said.

"OK, Eliot, take Happy with you."

Happy and I walked out to the old back road. The day before, on
the way to the beach, Mary Beth had pointed out the entrance to Old
Miss Gifford's home. It wasn't far, but Happy and I took our time.
My main worry was that Old Miss Gifford wouldn't believe me
about Mister McGillivery. And even if she did, she might have other
concerns. Would Bushwhacker use this to say that Point Aconi
was filled with a bunch of ignorant people who beat their children?
Would that give the politicians the excuse they needed to take the
land and kick everybody out? I'd never be able to come back to
Point Aconi again. And Earl would have to move away – away from
the place he loved. What about the *YNOT* and the attic with Great-
great-grandfather Steen's diary? What would become of all that?
I thought about my great-grandmother's picture above the bed.

"I'm watching you, boy." Minerva was her real name – that's what it said on her gravestone. "Help me do the right thing, Minerva," I whispered.

As I turned onto the long dirt lane that led up to Old Miss Gifford's place, I saw a lanky figure coming down the lane. It was Donnie McLeod. We both stopped and stood there frozen in our tracks. Happy snarled.

"I ain't gonna hurt you, Eye-talian," said Donnie.

"What? Why?" I asked.

"I don't feel like it just now," he said. "Anyhow, what are you doin' here?"

"I came to see Old Miss Gifford, and you?"

"Yeah, I just come from there," he said.

"Oh," I said, "are you in trouble again?"

"No!" he said loudly. "We wuz just talking, that's all."

"Did you tell her that you tried to kill me with a gaff?"

"Ha, I coulda hit you square in the head if I wanted to. I wuz just playing." I expected him to say something about Happy having to save me after I was screaming in the weeds, but he didn't say a word about it.

"What were you seeing Old Miss Gifford about?" I asked.

"What do you care?"

"I dunno," I said. "Just curious, I guess. Was she helpful?"

"Me pa kicked me off the boat again."

"Oh, I'm sorry, Donnie."

"Well, there's nothin' you can do about it, Eye-talian."

"I know," I said. "Just sorry, that's all."

He squinted at me in silence for a time. Sort of like he was trying to figure me out. Then he broke the silence and said, "Well, on your way, Eye-talian, and don't tell anybody you saw me here or I *will* whack you on the head with a gaff."

We crossed paths and waved. After twenty feet or so I looked back, but he was gone. I was beginning to think that Donnie was different when you talked to him one on one. Maybe he was one of

those kids who shows off when there's a group around. I knew a few kids like that in Lakefield.

On either side of the lane there were millions of wildflowers with honeybees buzzing about. After Happy and I passed through a stand of evergreens, I could see a tiny two-story cottage at the top of the lane and Miss Gifford's green truck parked beside it. If she saw me, I could say I had just come to pick flowers. As I inched closer, I noticed that the porch was edged with a white picket railing, topped with green flower boxes. Each was filled with purple and yellow blossoms that were spilling out in all directions.  I crept up the steps and could see a tidy white kitchen through the screen door. I stood there for a moment. I could still turn around and go back down the stairs. Instead, I closed my eyes and knocked softly.

"Just a minute," said a voice. I heard some noise, and after a while Old Miss Gifford's round body came into view.

"Eliot! Happy!" she said. "To what do I owe this great pleasure?"

"Oh, hello, Miss Gifford," I said.

"Call me Mabel," she said.

"Um, I've got sort of a problem."

"I'm glad you came," she said. "You make yourself comfortable on the porch, and I'll put on some tea." I looked around and saw that there was a white wicker table with two matching chairs. I sat down, and Happy found a comfortable spot on one of the steps. After about five minutes, Miss Gifford came out with a tray of tea and cookies.

"Gingersnap?" she asked.

"Oh, no thanks," I said. I was secretly hoping she'd ask again.

"Come now, you must try my gingersnaps."

"Oh, OK, if you insist."

"And tea?"

"Yes, please," I said.

"Milk and sugar?"

"Yes, please," I said.

When we were settled, she looked over and said, "So Eliot, what sort of problem is it?"

"Well, it's just that, um, I...I...I..." I was trying to come up with another story, any other story. "Um, was that Donnie I saw in your laneway?"

"Yes."

"What did he want?"

"Now Eliot, that's private. I will tell you that he's not a bad kid. Not really. Not deep down. He's having a tough time and just trying to figure things out. Same as you and me. Same as everybody. Was that what you came to see me about?"

"Well, no...it's just that, um, I...I...I..."

"Slow down and start again," she said.

"Mister McGillivery," I blurted, "he's beating Mary Beth! I saw the bruises at the beach and she told me, and there wasn't just one – there were lots of bruises."

I took a long breath and felt a wave of relief wash over me. I had let the genie out of the bottle, and I was just going to have to live with the consequences, whatever they might be. There was no turning back now, and that felt good.

"Oh, dear," said Old Miss Gifford, "and Mary Beth told you her father gave her the bruises?"

"Yes, but she told me not to tell anyone," I added.

Old Miss Gifford sucked her breath through her teeth and shook her head. "It's a terrible thing, Eliot, just terrible. But you did the right thing coming here. You know you did. This sort of thing shouldn't be hidden behind closed doors. Oh, poor Mary Beth!"

"She told me not to tell," I said again.

"I know, Eliot, but you must think, as I do, that this can't go on. Otherwise, why would you be here?"

"I know," I said.

"You leave it to me. First, I'll have a talk with Helen, that's

Mary Beth's mother. And then, Eliot, I'll let you know what comes of that."

"But I leave for Lakefield the day after tomorrow," I said.

"I'm going to speak to her right away. I'll go there first thing in the morning, when McGillivery is on the boat. This can't wait. I'll drop by Earl's tomorrow afternoon. Have you told Earl about this?" she asked.

"No," I said.

"Well, I think you'd better tell him. Tell him today," she said.

"OK," I said. "And one other thing, Miss Gifford...I mean Mabel, we overheard Mister McGillivery talking to the man from Bush-whacker Coal about selling their property."

"Really?" she said. "That property has been in Helen's family for generations. I think she'll have something to say about that too. Leave this to me."

When Happy and I arrived back, Earl was sitting on the steps.

"Feeling better?" he asked.

"No, Uncle Earl, I'm feeling pretty awful." When I saw the look of concern on his face, I realized he wasn't the mean old pirate I once thought he was. He was my uncle, and he cared about me. "I just visited Miss Gifford, and I have something that I need to tell you."

"What is it?" he asked.

"It's just that, well, when I was at the beach yesterday...with Timmy and Mary Beth...I saw some bruises on her."

"Yes," said Earl.

"I asked her how she got them, and...and well, she told me that her father beat her. And that it has happened a lot before."

"What?" said Earl, suddenly standing. "Why didn't you tell me?"

"Well, I was worried that if I told anybody, it would only make things worse for her. I thought about all of the bad things that might happen if I told, but I just couldn't keep it inside anymore. Because, well, Mary Beth is my friend." Then I started to cry.

I didn't mean to cry. I don't know why I did – it just came spilling out. I sat down on the grass, hung my head, and cried my guts out. First I felt Happy's cold nose nudge me on the arm, and then I felt Earl put his arm around my shoulder.

"You did the right thing, Eliot," he said.

"But Mary Beth said she'd get a beating for telling."

"We won't let that happen," said Earl. "That's why you went to see Mabel, isn't it?"

"Yes," I said.

"Good then. She'll know what to do."

"She's going to talk to Mary Beth's mother tomorrow morning," I said. "Then she's coming here after."

"Well, I think we'd better see how that plays out before anything gets said to Dermot. So tomorrow, on the boat, we'll just keep this under our hats, OK? And you probably shouldn't mention anything to Mary Beth either. No sense getting her upset."

"OK," I said as I gave him a hug. I remembered his bad back when he winced with pain. He didn't say anything this time; he just hugged me harder when I tried to let go. On top of everything else, I was mad at myself. Before I came to Point Aconi, I hadn't cried in about a year. And here I was, crying all over the place.

About a half an hour later, the gang arrived at Earl's back porch. "We're going down to the Sandy Spot to see what last night's storm brought us," said Mary Beth. She was carrying a big metal pot.

"What do you mean?" I said.

"You'll see! Tell Earl you're having dinner with us."

Earl didn't mind, but he reminded me that I could have dessert with him later – Butterscotch Ripple. So I pulled on my wellies, like the other kids had, and we started out. When we arrived at the Sandy Spot, Mary Beth and Jack grabbed two live lobsters and one blue crab that had been washed ashore by the storm. We all pitched in to make a circle of stones on the beach. Jack lit a fire in the center with some kindling that we borrowed from Earl's barn. Then Mary Beth filled the pot with seawater and set it on the stones over the fire. When the water started to boil, we threw in the live crab and the lobsters. The lobsters snapped their tails for a while and then all went quiet. After a few minutes, we carefully poured out the boiling water onto the beach and picked up our steaming dinner.

We sat on the rocks and cracked the shells open with large stones. We ate every last morsel. I even sucked the salty juice from a couple of the tiny lobster legs. Licking his lips, Jack jumped up and said, "Eliot, do you know the Newfie song?" Before I could answer, all of us linked arms, and we started to dance and sing:

I's the b'ye that builds the boat
And I's the b'ye that sails her
I's the b'ye that catches the fish
And brings them home to Liza.

Hip yer partner, Sally Thibault
Hip yer partner, Sally Brown
Fogo, Twillingate, Moreton's Harbour
All around the circle!

Sods and rinds to cover your flake
Cake and tea for supper
Codfish in the spring o' the year
Fried in maggoty butter.

I kept feeling sad when I looked over at Mary Beth, and yet it was a joyful time. We danced and sang that song again and again until we tripped each other up and collapsed into a tangle of boots and laughter. We stayed like that – a knot of arms and legs – until the laughter died down and the only sound was the surf rolling in.

Mary Beth broke the silence: "I'd better get back and help Ma." With that, we all got up and brushed the sand from our clothes. Mary Beth grabbed her pail, and we climbed up the rocks. As we passed the cemetery, I said a silent apology to Great-grandmother Purvis for peeing on her grave.

When we arrived at the split in the path, we said our goodbyes. Timmy said, "Wuh-we'll see you at the wuh-wharf tomorrow," and we gave each other a hug. When they were gone, Mary Beth and I walked along in silence until we reached Earl's.

"Tomorrow's your last day," she said. "You'll be leavin' the next morning."

"I know," I said. "Tomorrow's a big day." She kissed me, and as we hugged, I realized the next day might be the most difficult day Mary Beth had ever had. And all because of me. I didn't know it then, but that would be the last time Mary Beth kissed me that summer.

I didn't sleep well that night. In addition to everything else, I had started to miss my family and friends. I loved it here, but life in Point Aconi was so complicated. I wanted to feel like a kid again – just another kid who nobody noticed or took seriously.

15

During my last day on the *YNOT,* the overall feeling on the boat was pretty ordinary. There was less talk, but the three of us went about our business as usual. All that morning, I kept wondering if Old Miss Gifford was meeting with Mary Beth's mother at the exact moment that I was pulling up this cod or taking that bite of my sandwich. Maybe they were deciding what to do at the exact moment that Mister McGillivery was spitting out another wad of tobacco.

When we arrived back at the wharf, the gang was waiting.

"It's your last chance, Eliot b'ye," said Jack. "Are you going to swim out to the *Miss Louisa* with us today?"

"No," I said, "I think I'll leave that for next year."

"Sah-say you'll be buh-back again next year!" said Timmy.

"I hope so," I said. I didn't want to make a promise that I'd have to break.

That day, only Jack and Eddie swam over to the *Miss Louisa.* Mary Beth and Timmy hung back with me.

"Are you OK, Eliot?" asked Mary Beth. "You're too quiet."

"Huh?"

"Hello in there!" she said.

"Oh, I'm OK," I said.

"I nah-know what's wrong with him," said Timmy. "You're going to muh-miss us, right?"

"Yes, I am." I was surprised at how easily that came out. I would miss them; I would miss this whole crazy place.

"Mah-me too," said Timmy. "Wuh-will we read muh-more books next summer?" he asked.

"Yes," I said, "we have a whole library left to read."

After Jack and Eddie came back, we headed down the road.

We stopped at What's the Point, and I bought another round of chips for the gang. All the while, I had an awful feeling in my stomach. By then, Old Miss Gifford had probably finished her visit with Mary Beth's mother. I was worried about what might be waiting for Mary Beth when she arrived home. It was a good thing Mister McGillivery had gone into town to drink after fishing, as usual. He wouldn't hear a thing until he came home later that night.

When we finished our chips, I said goodbye to Penny, and the five of us headed for home.

We reached Jack and Eddie's place first. "Well," said Jack, "I guess this is goodbye then. Eddie and me are helping Pa salt cod tonight, so we can't come around. And I s'pose we'll be out on the boat before you leave tomorrow morning, eh?"

"Yeah, I s'pose," I said. "Thank you, guys. If I make it back next summer, I'll swim over to the *Miss Louisa*."

"Suuure you will," said Eddie.

"I will," I said. "I know I can do it."

"We'll make sure of it, b'ye," said Jack. "Safe travels, then."

"Goodbye, guys," I said.

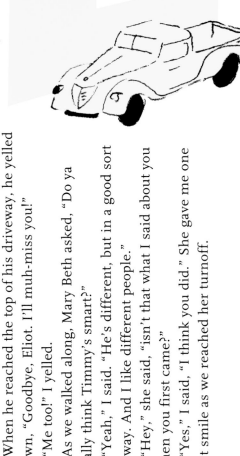

A few minutes later, we reached Timmy's place. "Will ya wuh-write?" he asked.

"I will," I said. "And, Timmy, don't let anybody tell you you're slow or dumb or anything like that. You're one of the smartest guys I know."

"Really?" he asked. He looked like he might cry.

"Yes, really," I said. We hugged before he turned and walked away.

When he reached the top of his driveway, he yelled down, "Goodbye, Eliot. I'll muh-miss you!"

"Me too!" I yelled.

As we walked along, Mary Beth asked, "Do ya really think Timmy's smart?"

"Yeah," I said. "He's different, but in a good sort of way. And I like different people."

"Hey," she said, "isn't that what I said about you when you first came?"

"Yes," I said, "I think you did." She gave me one last smile as we reached her turnoff.

"I'll sneak out tonight," she said, "and meet you on Earl's lawn. About nine o'clock?"

"Yes, OK."

As I walked up Earl's driveway, I could hear people talking. When I reached the top, I saw Old Miss Gifford and Earl sitting on the back porch steps. I also saw Uncle Earl's hand on Old Miss Gifford's knee. When he heard my footsteps on the gravel, he quickly pulled it away.

"Oh, hello, Eliot," said Earl.

"Hi."

"Come sit with us," said Mabel as she patted a place next to her on the steps.

I sat down and asked how the meeting with Mary Beth's mother went. "I can't lie and tell you that it all went well," said Mabel, "but Helen agreed to a temporary plan."

"What is it?" I asked.

"Mary Beth is going to come and live with me for a while. In the meantime, we'll try to get help for the McGillivery family."

"What will happen?"

"I'm not sure, Eliot. With the right kind of help, Mister McGillivery might learn to change his ways. And if that doesn't happen, he'll have to leave, or Helen and the kids may have to go somewhere else. For now, we'll just have to take it one day at a time," she said.

"But if Bushwhacker finds out about this, won't they use that against people in Point Aconi?"

"No, Eliot. That would be a very stupid thing for them to try to do, and we won't let it happen."

"Will you join us for dinner, Mabel?" asked Earl.

"No, I can't. I'm going over to pick up Mary Beth now. She's probably packing as we speak. I want her to have a bit of time to settle in."

"I understand," said Earl. Before Old Miss Gifford left, Earl whispered something into her ear. She grabbed his arm and smiled. I was starting to think that they were much more than just friends. When Old Miss Gifford's green pickup pulled away, Earl looked over at me and asked if toasted bacon, lettuce, and tomato sandwiches would work for dinner.

"Yes, of course," I said. "You know how much I love your cooking."

Uncle Earl gave me the biggest grin I'd ever seen.

After dinner I started packing up my things. I folded everything into the suitcase except my pajamas and the clothes I was going to wear the next day. Earl had made two leather straps with buckles to hold my suitcase closed. I looked up at the portrait of Great-grand-mother Purvis and noticed a sort of mild smile for the first time. She didn't seem so stern or judgmental anymore. I was thinking about how much had changed, when I heard a loud rapping at the back screen door.

"Earl," said a gruff voice. "Earl, it's me, Dermot. Where are you, b'ye?" I snuck into the kitchen to listen. I heard Earl descending the stairs from the attic.

"What is it, Dermot?" said Earl. "Are you drunk again?"

"Never mind dat," he said. "I come here to give dat little Eliot a hiding he won't soon fergit."

"That's not going to happen," said Earl.

"Are ya takin' his side now? Did ya know the little frigger said I wuz beatin' on my Mary Beth?"

"I know all about it," said Earl.

"And you believe the little frig?"

"I do," said Earl.

"Well don't you 'spect me to show up on yer old YNOT then."

"I'm good with that," said Earl.

"OK then. Tell the little frig somethin' for me, will ya?" said Mister McGillivery.

"What's that?" asked Earl.

"Tell him that it would be a real shame if he came back again next summer – I ain't saying, but he isn't much of a swimmer..."

"Is that a threat?" asked Earl.

"I ain't saying nuthin'," said Mister McGillivery.

"If you've got nothing to say, then be on your way," said Earl.

After Mister McGillivery left, I joined Earl on the porch.

"If I come back to Point Aconi next summer," I asked, "will Mister McGillivery try to hurt me?"

"No," said Earl. "He's a very troubled man, but he wouldn't go that far. I hope he gets the help that Mabel was talking about. He'll see how wrong he is."

"Who will you use for a helper on the *YNOT* now?"

"I'm not sure, Eliot. Maybe Girly was right all along. Maybe I'm getting too old for this – too old to start over again with a new helper. On top of it all, my back and knees are giving me trouble. With Dermot gone, this might be the right time to pack it all in and move to town."

"No!" I yelled. "You can't leave Point Aconi. What would you do in town? What about Mabel and the rest of the people here? You can't sell your place to Bushwhacker. If you did that, everybody in Point Aconi would sell. Bushwhacker would ruin it forever!"

"But I thought you didn't like it here, Eliot."

"I love Point Aconi!"

"Who would I get to help me on the *YNOT*?"

"What about Donnie McLeod? He's available."

"Donnie McLeod? His father says he's useless. And didn't he bully you all summer?"

"I think he just needs another chance, sir. Why don't you talk to Miss Gifford about him?"

"Well, I could maybe give him a try. As you know, I have a certain fondness for lost causes." He looked at me with a twinkle in his eye and I wondered if I was one of his lost causes.

"You'd better get to bed, Eliot. Girly will be here to pick you up early. Are you packed?"

"Mostly," I said.

"I'll see you in the morning, then," he said.

At nine o'clock that night, I snuck out to meet Mary Beth.

There was a full moon and not many stars.

I waited for over an hour, but she never showed up. I felt sick. I was sure that she hated me for revealing her secret. She told me about the bruises in confidence and begged me not to tell anybody. I snuck back into my room, got into bed, and curled up into a little ball.

The next morning, Earl, Happy, and I waited for Grandmother McNeil on the back porch steps. When her car pulled in, the scene must have looked very familiar. Earl and Happy, sitting there, with their intense brown eyes, squinting in the sun. Except this time, I was in the middle.

"Well, look at that," said Grandmother McNeil. "See no evil, hear no evil, and speak no evil. Let's go, boy," she said as she jabbed her key into the trunk lock. "Well, boy, did you talk to your great-uncle about leaving Point Aconi, hmm? Did you let him know how much better his life would be in town? I bet you can't wait to get back to Lakefield, eh? Back to civilization." I looked over at Earl. He winked at me and gave me the shush sign with his finger.

"No, Grandmother, it never came up."

"Never came up? Didn't you miss your television and your friends and your father's cooking? Didn't you miss civilization?"

"No, not really, Grandmother."

"Oh, Eliot! What am I going to do with you two? Well, get moving,

I don't want to hang around here long." Earl lugged the heavy green suitcase over to the car and heaved it into the trunk.

He reached into his pocket and pulled out a small package that was wrapped in newspaper.

"This is for you," he said. "Open it on the plane. And this is also for you." He handed me a yellow envelope with my name neatly printed in pencil on the front. "Mary Beth came by earlier this morning and asked me to give it to you."

"Thank you." I gave him a hug. Then I got down on my knees and hugged Happy. I hugged him for a long time.

Finally, Grandmother McNeil broke in and said, "C'mon, boy!"

I didn't let go right away. In fact, I kept hugging Happy for a while longer. When Grandmother McNeil let out a big long sigh, I whispered into the dog's ear, "Don't forget me, Happy. I know you're old, but please be here when I come back." At that, he gave me one last lick on the nose, and I let him go. Earl had already opened the passenger door. I climbed in.

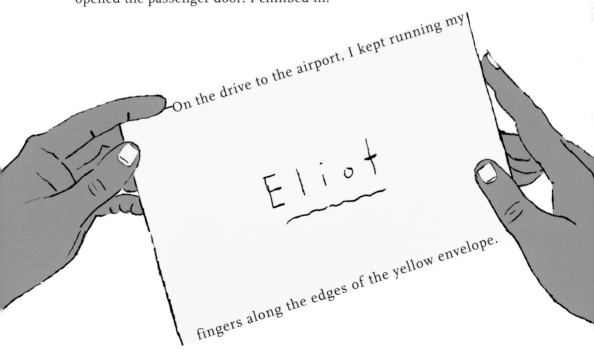

On the drive to the airport, I kept running my fingers along the edges of the yellow envelope.

Eliot

"So," said Grandmother McNeil, "I can't quite believe that you had a good time in that backwater."

"It's not a backwater," I said. "It's my favorite place in the whole world."

"Eliot, please," she said. "What do you know about the world?"

"I know more than you think," I said firmly. I must have used the right tone because she didn't say too much else.

When we arrived at the airport in Halifax, Grandmother McNeil helped me drag the suitcase from the trunk and onto the sidewalk.

"Well, Eliot, you didn't help me any this summer, but I can see that you helped yourself. And that's something, I guess. Goodbye, dear, I'm late," she said as she gave me a dry kiss on the forehead. With that, she and her golden Pontiac glided away.

After checking in, I boarded the plane. The very same stewardess greeted me at the door but didn't seem to recognize me. "Seat 22 – you're all the way at the back, sir," she said.

When I got to my seat, the first thing I did was rip open the letter.

Dear Eliot,

I'm sorry that I didn't come last night. I was really mad at you. I told you not to tell.

I'm really worried about my mom. What will she do without me? What about my brothers and sisters?

I've been crying a lot, but Old Miss Gifford is really nice. We had gingersnaps. She thinks you did the right thing, but I don't know if I can ever tell you another secret. Even if I can't tell you any more secrets, I wish you could have stayed for a little while longer.

I hope you can come back to Point Aconi. I still have your mermaid towel.

Will you write to me?

Mary Beth

I rubbed my thumb over the red hearts she drew on the border of the letter.

Then I opened the present from Earl. It was my Great-great-grandfather Steen's diary. I knew that it meant a lot to Earl. His mother Minnie had given it to him. And I knew then that I would keep the diary safe so I could pass it along to the right person one day. Who knows, maybe I'll have a kid of my own. If I do, I'll ship him off to Point Aconi for the summer. The thought of my mother being right all along made me wince, but I couldn't wait to see her. And my dad. I even missed my sister a little.

At that point I saw the stewardess coming down the aisle with drinks and peanuts. When she got close to me, she stared at me for a while.

"Say," she said finally, "aren't you the same kid who traveled with us a couple months back?"

I took the time to politely turn away to blow my nose and wipe my eyes. Then I looked at her and said: "I don't think so. I'm a whole other person now."

I grinned at her,

and she grinned back at me.

THE END.

ABOUT THE AUTHOR

Frank Viva is an award-winning artist and designer who lives
in Toronto with his family. Many decades ago he spent summers in
Point Aconi, Nova Scotia – and while the story in this book is
entirely fictional, Frank's memories of the place inspired it.
Viva's other books include the *New York Times* Best Illustrated
Children's Book selection *Along a Long Road*, the Parents' Choice
Award winner *A Long Way Away*, and TOON's Cybils award-winning
A Trip to the Bottom of the World. His art has appeared in many
places, including regularly on the cover of *The New Yorker*.
Visit him online at vivaandco.com

Created with the generous support of
Julia Viva, Camille Viva, Mia Viva, Todd Temporale
and the talented practitioners at moveable.com.